I0678061

ALIEN STARSWARM

Salvatore commands the battleship *Endymion*, a cruiser ready-made for trouble—a cruiser with the dubious honor of being the lead ship for the mercenary forces of Count Sforza. Salvatore has seen his share of battles and fought them bravely, too. So he doesn't hesitate when the beautiful Princess Hatari pleads for his help.

The Princess wants to regain her throne on the planet Melchior, and Salvatore is sworn to assist her. It may be even more than Salvatore can accomplish, however, for the deadly race known as the Balderdash has taken over Melchior, and now, even his own men have turned against him.

Bred to fight, he accepts the challenge!

Borgo Press Books by ROBERT SHECKLEY

Alien StarSwarm: A Science Fiction Tale

ALIEN STARSWARM

A SCIENCE FICTION TALE

ROBERT SHECKLEY

THE BORGO PRESS
MMX

ALIEN STARSWARM

Copyright © 1990 by Robert Sheckley
Copyright © 2010 by Gail Sheckley, Executor of the Estate of Robert Sheckley

FIRST EDITION

Published by Wildside Press LLC

www.wildsidebooks.com

PROLOGUE

Salvatore stretched in front of the spaceship control panel. He yawned.

"Tired, Boss?" asked Toma, his spider robot.

"Only bored, Toma. Only bored."

He'd joined the StarSwarm fleet to see action and danger. No one had told him there would be periods of waiting that would test his thin patience. How could anyone expect a sixteen-year-old commander to sit idle? He eased forward and flipped a button. A ray of light flicked through the sky.

"Boss! You could blast another vessel to Stagmall and gone!"

"I need action, Toma. I only want to tear up a few ships or maybe sack a planet or two."

"I'd save my energy if I were you," said Toma. "You know nothing stays quiet around here for long."

CHAPTER ONE

Salvatore paced up and down the wide, carpeted area in front of the huge, curving windows of the battleship *Endymion*. Through them, he could see a splendid view of the Semiramis region of Space from a distance of a mere 1.3 light-years. In this dense region near the Galactic Center, a million pinpoints of light flared and glowed in colors ranging from pale violet through angry red. Sal wasn't interested in the spectacle now, though at another time, it would have thrilled his sixteen-year-old heart.

He was watching for the first sign of his squadron returning, even though he knew the radar would pick them up long before he could make them out visually.

"Still no sign of them?" he asked Toma, his spider robot assistant, who was on the other side of the Command Room near the radar readout.

"You know I'd tell you as soon as I picked up a signal," the little robot said. "Calm down, Boss. You know they're all right."

"Just keep watching that screen," Sal said.

The spider robot waved two tentacles in a curious gesture that was his equivalent of a nod. He had a body mass about the size and shape of an aluminum beer keg, rounded at both ends. Extruding from his body were a dozen tentacle-like limbs, made of a flexible gray metal. He could extrude more limbs as circumstances required.

No one knew how the spider-robots came into existence. They were, as their name implied, a novel cross between living spider and non animate robot. They were usually colored medium gray or slate blue, though a few species were orange with blue checks. It was not known what these different colors might signify.

Human explorers first found the spider robots on the planet Stagma II. They already had an advanced mechanical civilization, although their development had stopped short of Space flight. The spider robots were eager to cooperate with other intelligent species, and were often taken on interstellar journeys as data assistants.

"Anything yet?" Sal asked.

"Not yet, Boss. Don't worry!"

"I can't help but worry," Salvatore said. "Some of my men are new to Space conflicts. Even though the engagement I sent them to didn't look like it would offer much resistance...."

"A piece of cake," the robot said. "You said so yourself."

"But you can never tell in advance. Not really. I should have gone with them."

Toma crossed two tentacles in a negative gesture. "You know the rules. You are bound by your contract to Sforza to send them into at least one action under their second-in-command, Dick Fogarty, so their decisions and actions can be appraised for future leadership positions."

"I know, I know," Salvatore said "But maybe Star Pass Nine wasn't the right engagement to send them to."

"It was the best small action to come along in months," the robot pointed out. "Another month without sending them into an engagement and you would have been in violation of contract."

"Still, maybe I should have gone along."

"Boss, you did the right thing. They can take care of themselves."

"They're just kids at heart," Salvatore said, evidently unaware of the irony of such words issuing from the lips of one who had just celebrated his sixteenth birthday.

"That's because they've taken the Immaturity Option," Toma said. "It's the best conditioning for space ship fighter pilots. It makes them dashing and courageous. But also, if you will excuse the thought, a little reckless."

Salvatore shook his head. "It's a weird world when sixteen-year-olds command adult men. But what the hell, that's the system. I didn't invent it. I know they'll be okay. But where in hell are they?"

§

It seemed as if it would go on forever: Salvatore and the spider robot, alone in the darkened Battle

Command Station, reading the dials, waiting. But things can change fast in Space. One moment everything was going along as usual, with all instruments reading in normal range, and with Salvatore sitting in the big command chair, nervous, bored and worried about his men and wondering where he would take his leave time next year.

The next moment, a light flashed on the Communication Board, and an alarm went off. It could have been a false summons, since the alarms did go off from time to time for no discernable reason. But this felt like something different to Sal. The alarm had an emergency feel about it, accompanied as it was by the strident burr of the buzzer and the red light flashing on the board.

"That's them!" Sal cried.

But the spider robot said in a cheery voice, "It's not the battle group."

"Who could it be, then?"

"Don't know, but it looks like you got a visitor, Boss!"

The robot pointed to the screen with one slender tentacle. The blip showed a spaceship of unknown origin, coming toward the *Endymion* at full speed.

It was an awkward time to receive callers on a battleship without defenders, with only a sixteen-year-old commander and a spider robot there to hold the fort.

Of course, Salvatore was not just anybody. He had a Commander's license in the Sforza Condottieri forces, and he had been top of his class on the Battle Organ the year he graduated from the Uni Prep war college. He was one tough sixteen-year-old, and he was ready for trouble.

At this time in the Semiramis region, no inhabited planet had a Space navy of its own. The great military houses of the Condottieri with their freelance armies did most of the fighting, hiring themselves out to either side, battling other Condottieri bands who had signed contracts with their enemies. As a partial check on their powers, Condottieri were not supposed to live on planets they worked for.

It was not an ideal system, but it had worked well enough up to this point. Salvatore, as officer on the scene, was supposed to make up his own mind about matters when they came up. Correct decisions could mean advancement; incorrect ones could result in unpleasantness, including condemnation on charges of treason, and then, summary execution. Often the execution came first, and the trial later. The Sforza and other Condottieri families took few chances.

§

Salvatore didn't bother with the Battle Organ. Not for one ship. Instead he toggled the satellite's laser guns to the ON position and sat up straight in the command chair. He was of normal height for a boy of sixteen, but the chair had been padded to raise him and give him a better view. He was a tall, skinny kid, with a head of unruly orange-red curls. His eyes were an intense cold blue.

His guns locked onto the target. Before him, through the curving window, was the unsurpassed view of the night sky stretching as towards the constellation Agamemnon in the Semiramis region.

There was usually a lot of action in this part of the galaxy. This was where the Big Bang was said to have begun, starting the human race on its still unended career. In this region, inhabited planets were more packed than countries on a map of old Earth. One thousand and seventy-one planetary civilizations traded, took holidays on each other's worlds, and sometimes went to war with each other. Scattered through the entire region were the Condottieri, independent mercenary battle groups who hired themselves out to planets without StarSwarms of their own. Politics changed quickly out here. Salvatore's mission was to monitor the flow of events in this region, and look for suitable fighting opportunities for his Battle Group.

Salvatore put out a trace on the alarm. Soon a flashing LED line came up on the navigation screen. It showed something moving toward them.

"It's coming," Salvatore muttered to himself. "Closing fast."

"It should have started a braking orbit by now." Toma the robot said. "It's coming directly toward us.

"Scared?" Salvatore asked.

"Of course not. Spider robots have very little instinct for survival. It doesn't matter to me if the ship destroys this entire battleship."

"Thanks a lot," Salvatore said.

"No insult intended."

Salvatore studied the moving LED line. "Maybe the pilot doesn't dare slow down."

"Why not?"

"See those faint tracings of lights behind him on the screen? Looks like ships in hot pursuit, doesn't it?"

"Yes," the robot said. "That is the most logical explanation."

Salvatore studied the screen. There were about a dozen blips following the spaceship. On the basis of their velocity and mass, he was certain they were short range spaceships, probably from a nearby planet. No more detailed identification was possible at this range. The leading spaceship, trying to pull away from its pursuers, was closing fast on Salvatore's battleship.

"Try to raise the pilot on radio," Salvatore said.

The robot turned some dials, fiddled with a rheostat, and touched a filter button.

"No answer yet. This guy's coming in so fast, I figure he's set up a magnetic resonance that's blocking radio waves, or maybe he's shut down the whole electromagnetic spectrum."

"He's going to have to slow down pretty soon," Salvatore said. "Or go through us."

"He's just begun deceleration," the robot said.

Salvatore turned on the long distance displacer cannon and set the sights for maximum range. The spaceship kept on coming, its blip swelling on the screen.

"So what are you going to do?" the robot asks.

Salvatore didn't answer. There was a sudden burst of static from the big speakers mounted on either side of the control board. A light display panel showed a series of squiggles, then went to black.

"Make sense out of that for me," Salvatore said.

The robot quickly adjusted switches. The sound came through again, cleaned, filtered, amplified and slowed. This time, the message was unmistakable.

"Help! I am being attacked!" The message was in Intergab, one of the main trading languages in the Semiramis portion of Space. Judging by the intonation, though poorly reproduced by the space radio, Sal guessed the speaker was female.

"A call for help!" the robot said.

Salvatore shrugged. "It doesn't matter. I have to follow the rules. Punch up Standard Response 1."

The robot did so. The message went out. "Please identify yourself."

"Spaceship *Leitra*, Princess Hatari commanding. I am being pursued by two Balderdash Attack craft. Please let me take refuge on your battleship."

"The Balderdash," Sal said. "Who are the Balderdash?"

Toma performed the odd series of clicks to tune into the Galactic Information Channel.

"A newly discovered race," he said after a while. "Not much is known about them."

The woman's voice on the radio came through, "Didn't you hear me? I need help!"

"I guess we've heard that one before," the robot said.

"I guess we have," Sal said. "Do you think one of the other Condottieri chiefs could be trying to pull a fast one on us?"

"The closest Condottieri are the Borgia squadron on South Myna Star Salient. They have shown no recent signs of bellicosity."

"So this might be a genuine distress call. Well.... Transmit Standard Response 2."

The robot broadcast, "Do not come any closer to this ship! It is the property of the Sforza Condottieri. Only ships with legitimate contracts with a Sforza Battle Group can claim protection. Back off, or I will be forced to fire."

On the big plotting screen, Salvatore could see the light dot representing the spaceship *Leitra*, closely pursued by two smaller ships. A ripple of light crossed the screen. Firing had commenced.

"My pursuers are firing on me!" Princess Hatari radioed.

"I'm sorry about that," Salvatore radioed back. "But there's nothing I can do about it. However, I must point out you are approaching this battleship's protective shield. Within the shield is Sforza space. Trespassing is forbidden. Break off from your course immediately or I will commence firing."

"But I'm seeking help! I'm being attacked!"

"That is no concern of mine! Get out of Sforza space before I slam a torpedo into you!"

"Darn it, I have a right to be here! I have a contract for Sforza support and services!"

Salvatore looked at the robot. The robot made a shrug-like movement with its tentacles.

"Why didn't you mention this earlier?" Sal asked.

"I had my hands full maneuvering this ship," Hatari replied.

"What is your contract number?"

A telltale light on the screen flashed, showing that the ship had penetrated the outermost defenses of the Sforza planetoid.

"Don't shoot," Hatari said. "I'll have to look it up."

Five seconds passed. Hatari's ship continued to move in toward the planetoid.

Salvatore was tracking the ship through simulated gun-sights. He locked the battleship's guns onto the ship. He said to the robot, "On my mark, begin count-down to zero, and then fire."

"Not so fast!" Hatari said. "I told you. I've got the contract number around here somewhere!"

"...eight, seven, six..."

"Wait, it must be in the accounts receivable file!"

"...three, two..."

"Here it is! 77089—aa23!"

Salvatore looked at the robot. "Well?"

"It's a legitimate contract number."

More lights flashed on the control board as the ship penetrated the second line of defenses. There was one more line left to pass.

Salvatore turned off the guns. He said, "Put your ship into a parking orbit and 'port over here immediately."

"I'm coming right over," Hatari said. "Signing off."

CHAPTER TWO

Half an hour later, the spider robot announced, in his most formal manner, "Princess Mary Jane Hatari."

The spaceport entry dilated. In strode a tall, attractive young woman clad in snakeskin boots and a large billowing green cloak. She wore a diadem from which glittered a single enormous sapphire. Her features were bold and imperious, yet they fit current definitions of humanoid beauty. She glared at Salvatore suspiciously.

"Who are you?"

"I'm the Sforza representative," Salvatore said.

"But you're only a kid!" She stared at him hard. "An attractive kid, but still, only a kid."

"Maybe I am," Salvatore said. "But this kid has saved your bacon, and has the power to put you right out again so your fat is in the fire."

"I didn't know Sforza hired commanders so young."

"Sixteen is the ideal age for a Condottieri Battleship Commander," Sal told her. "Our reflexes are at their peak. The job of making and breaking alliances is still of interest to a young person like me. It will get pretty stale soon. Then I'll move on to something else. But that's enough about me. What about you?"

"I am from the planet Excelsus," Hatari said. "I am the offspring of a star line and graduate of an alpha program in leadership."

Sal nodded. He had heard of Excelsus, a planet whose main export was rulers for the many worlds who wanted them.

"So you've been through the Excelsian Development Program?"

"I have," Princess Hatari said. "I have a copy of my personality profile in the spaceship if you'd care to see it. It shows that I am intelligent, incorruptible, impartial, very good looking, and suited in every way to rule Melchior."

"Melchior? Is that around here somewhere?"

"It's in the northeast quadrant of Semiramis, a small planet inhabited by a race called the Simi."

"Did the Simi ask for you, or are you to be imposed on them?"

"What kind of talk is that?" the princess asked crossly. "They jumped at the chance of being ruled by a genuine Excelsian princess. They agreed to a five year contract, with options." She paused. "I was to start today."

"What happened?"

Princess Hatari sighed. She looked around for a place to sit. Sal gestured her to the overstuffed chair floating inches above the floor near her. The Princess settled into it, steadying it as it dipped under her weight.

"That's better," she said. "You wouldn't have a cup of tea, would you?"

"I'll get it at once," Toma said, hurrying out of the room.

The princess sighed and settled back in her chair.

"No sooner did I get to Melchior than I found that an alien race had come to the planet during the ten days of subjective time it took me to get there. They were big, tall creatures, ten feet or more in height, very skinny, with Jurassic mouthfolds and triangular eyes. They had a very nasty expression, and were not at all genteel. I learned they were the Balderdash."

"What were these Balderdash doing there?" Sal asked.

The spider robot came hurrying back in with tea for the princess, and Ovaltine for Sal. He had brought a plate of cookies too, and the Princess munched one.

"My, this is good! I haven't had a cookie like this since I left Excelsus!"

"Our autochef is a genius," Sal said. "You must come over for dinner this evening, when my men have returned. But you were telling me about the Balderdash."

"I never did find out who, if anyone, had invited them to Melchior," Princess Hatari said. "But they claimed to have been elected to Planetary Overlordship by open plebiscite on the planet."

"Did you see the tallies?" Sal asked.

"I asked to see them. They refused. We had some words. When I pointed out they were in violation of several interstellar covenants, they made threatening statements. When I returned to my ship, they followed.

They have been chasing me ever since."

"Thank you for this information," Sal said. "I will consider what you have told me."

"But will you help me?"

"I suppose I will. But I will give you a more definite answer later."

The princess retired to her spaceship, which was anchored to the landing platform behind one of the giant battleship's dorsal fins. Sal decided to confer with Toma.

"So are you going to help her?" the spider robot asked.

"I believe I will," Salvatore said. "As chief bubaldar for this station. I am empowered to enter into contracts. The princess has a wealthy sponsor. He'll pay plenty for me to put her on the throne."

"Do you think you'll be able to oust the Balderdash?"

Sal's eyes held a dangerous glint. But his voice was mild as he said, "I think I can bring it off."

Sal finished his tea and went back to the main Computing Center aboard the ship. There was a signal awaiting him. It was from someone Sal had lost touch with a long time ago: Alfonso, his Petri-dish brother from the Zygote Factory on Terra XI.

CHAPTER THREE

Sal grabbed for the radio transmitter. "Al! Is that really you?"

"You bet it is," Alfonso's familiar voice came back.

"But what are you doing out here?"

"Checking out mineral deposits. I saw on Recent Postings that you were out in this region. I'm only a couple thousand miles away. I thought we might get together."

"Yes, let's!" Sal said. "Do you want to come here or shall I go to your ship?"

"I think you've got better facilities."

Sal decided that Alfonso was probably manning a one-man class B Minerals Explorer Probe. The amenities wouldn't be much on a workhorse like that, whereas Sal was commander of a star class Battleship, one that had all the amenities expected of someone showing the Sforza battle flag.

Alfonso would be impressed. It would give Sal a chance to show off a bit. That wasn't very nice, he told himself. But he forgave himself in advance. He'd get back to self-discipline after Alfonso left.

Alfonso's stubby little ship locked onto one of the

battleship's entry ports. Soon Alfonso came through the port. He was a good-looking boy, exactly Sal's age, and he was wearing a high-fashion black explorer's tunic with tailored riding breeches. Goggles were draped casually around his neck, the mark of a deep-space man. But Sal couldn't get his eyes off that tunic. It had zippers everywhere, like the pictures of the airplane pilots who fought Earth's ancient wars in the skies. Sal felt a twinge of jealousy. He decided he'd get himself a tunic just like it, only with more zippers.

Alfonso was almost half a head taller than he was, though their height had been identical when they were both five years old. That was almost eleven years ago, back in the playground attached to the zygote factory.

The earliest thing Sal remembered was his birth place, Zygote Factory 122a on Drina 12. He could still smell the dusty factory odors; see the fluorescent lighting, full and without focus; and hear the soft hum of machinery nurturing the thousands of developing zygotes.

Alfonso had been in the Petri dish on his left hand side, the final one in the long row. That made Alfonso a close brother to him, especially since he had no brother on his right hand side, an oversight of factory planning that might have been responsible for Sal's bouts of moodiness.

Of course, all the zygotes from 122a were his brothers, technically speaking. But with Alfonso it was different, more special. He liked Alfonso and wanted Alfonso to like him. Sometimes he also hated Alfonso and wanted to best him. It made for an interesting relationship.

After early development, the two boys had played together. Sal remembered the enormous playground at 122a, green with Ev'ergreen, a grass substitute made of recycled plastics, a substance that never needed cutting and was considered superior to the real thing. The two boys had played the usual games at that time, based on war and business, mankind's two chief concerns. Alfonso was always physically bolder, though Sal was the more clever of the two.

Early on in life, they had both been selected for advanced studies. Sal's skill at electronic games had guaranteed him entry to the yearly military-management draft, when lucky boys and girls with good intelligence and superior hand-eye coordination were selected by the Condottieri. They learned to lead older troops, men of twenty to thirty, already past their prime, reflex-wise, but good enough for handling one man fighters in the formations known as StarSwarms. After a brief period as a free agent, Sal had signed with Sforza, one of the biggest of the independent warlords, who controlled half a dozen mercenary battle groups in his region of space near the Galactic Center.

Alfonso had taken a different path. He hadn't been interested in war. He had signed for the Management Resources Program with Substances Ltd., a huge conglomerate that had mining interests on many different planets. Alfonso decided to specialize in the Rare British Explorations Division, where his boldness and lack of self-reflection would be useful traits. The boys hadn't met since graduation from dear old 122a.

"Well, Sal," Alfonso said. "You look like you're keeping well."

"Can't complain," Salvatore said. "What about yourself?"

Alfonso shrugged. He got up from the chair and walked to the sideboard. There he poured himself a fruit drink. Already he had the serious, no-nonsense look that characterized so many of the Business people. He was a good-looking boy, straight nose, regular features. His mouth, even at the age of sixteen, was tight. He looked handsome, self-contained, unflappable, and a little wistful, like a child peering out of a hard boy's face.

Sal, on the other hand, was more immediately emotional. Red-haired, with freckled skin that burned easily, he felt things directly, and he acted on his intuitions. This was considered a good quality in a battle group commander. One had to have the right instincts to run a battle group.

"So what do you do." Alfonso asked, "working for a Condottieri?"

"The usual military stuff," Sal said. "Putting down rebellions. Helping one side or the other. Occasionally something interesting comes up." He poured Alfonso another fruit juice and said, with exaggerated unconcern "Like now, I'm going to take on a job of restoring a princess to her throne."

"You're kidding," Alfonso said. "I didn't know they

still had princesses ruling planets."

"Better believe it, and she's a real one, from Excelsus. But it's going to take some action to get this thing done right."

"Will it be dangerous?" asked Alfonso, a little note of awe in his voice that pleased Sal very much.

"Oh, I suppose so," Sal said offhandedly, "But I've got a good bunch of lads here under my command. We're going to go in and do it right." He felt a swell of satisfaction as he spoke. He could see how impressed Alfonso was by it all.

"Which planet is it?" Alfonso asked.

"Melchior. It's a small green one in the Cygne system."

"I know the place! I'm going there to check out the mineral rights for Substances Ltd!"

"Then I'll see you there," Sal said.

"Wow, that's really great," Alfonso said. "I hope you'll give me a good deal on mineral rights, if this place turns out to have anything valuable. It'll look good to my company."

"Consider it done," Sal said magnanimously.

Alfonso had never been aboard a star class battleship. He was especially interested in the War Simulations Room, where the main Battle Organ was located. He looked at that instrument with awe. To operate it, one sat back in a reclining lounge-chair. The Battle Organ was lowered over the operator, a half-sphere surrounding his head and shoulders. Over three hundred instruments could be reached with minimum movements of arm and hand. There were entire sets of data gloves within easy reach, each controlling different arrays of offensive and defensive weapons. Alfonso knew that these allowed Sal to control different parts of the attack operation.

A computer could have been programmed to run the Battle Organ. But the matter of intuition that lay behind choice was a human gift, not a cybernetic one. Sal could beat any computer operated war game played against him.

Playing a game of war and fighting a real one were not just similar; with modem weaponry, they were identical. In both, there was the god-like feeling of controlling complicated matters with an effortless ease. In actuality, running a battle simulator, even for a few minutes, was extremely taxing. No one could do it for long. The Battle Organ was provided with a cut-in operating program which could take over when the human operator took his few moments of involuntary rest.

With the Battle Organ, one never saw any blood or torn or scorched flesh. It could be dialed up on the screen, but it wasn't necessary. Not that Sal was squeamish. But it helped to play the game when he could keep it impersonal.

CHAPTER FOUR

Sal was trying to relax—a difficult task as his men still hadn't returned—when he received an urgent signal from Toma, asking the commander to visit him as soon as convenient. Sal went to confer with Toma in his quarters.

On their own planet, the spider robots lived in caves where they spun vast communal webs. All of them took turns repairing old web and creating new web. Onboard the *Endymion*, Toma had a room to himself. It was filled entirely with gossamer filaments of web. Once a spider robot was in his web, he fell immediately into a deep, trancelike sleep. It was almost impossible to wake him before his own internal time clock clicked over to waking mode.

Opening the door, Sal saw what looked at first like swirling mist. After a moment his vision adjusted and he saw it for what it was—gossamer-light filaments, spun to a great fineness, and filling the room entirely. There was a hint of furniture, but this too was constructed out of filament. Toma had spun a chair for Sal, and had applied hardener so it wouldn't collapse under him. On the walls, there were portraits of Toma's parents, also done in filament and colored with different dyes. The room had a misty, faraway and long-ago sort of look, as though Sal were seeing it in a dream.

"Come in, sit down," Toma said. "I have already brewed your favorite Ovaltine drink for you. And perhaps you'd like to try these." He picked up a plate from a low filament table and extended it to Sal on one tentacle. There was an embroidered cloth over the plate, made of gossamer with bright threads of red and green running through it.

"What is it?" Sal asked.

"Look for yourself," Toma said. Sal removed the cloth. Beneath, he saw small circular objects, black in color, made up of two circles pasted together with a white substance.

Sal picked one up, sniffed it, cautiously bit into it. He burst into an astonished grin.

"Oreos!" he cried. "And the genuine formula, too! Toma, where did you get them? Genuine Oreos haven't been seen for at least two hundred years."

"I came across the recipe recently while I was monitoring the Spider Robot CB Net. One of our archaeologists dug it up on a recent trip to Earth. Is it good?"

"Extremely good," Sal said. "I only wish you could taste one for yourself."

"I wish so too, Boss. But you know we spider robots eat only metals. I will have a little candied copper filigree just to keep you company."

They munched together companionably for a while, boy and spider robot in the web-filled storeroom. Then

Toma asked. "Are you really going to help Princess Hatari, Boss?"

"I am," Sal said flatly. "I don't like what I've heard of the Balderdash. And I have the right to enter into an independent contract."

"Only," Toma pointed out, "if no previous contract exists."

"The only contract that exists is one between Princess Hatari and Sforza. She told us that herself."

"I'm afraid the princess exaggerated a bit," Toma said.

"What do you mean?" Sal asked.

"I took the liberty of accessing the aforementioned contract on the Warlord Agreements Database. A contract exists, commander, but it is not between Princess Hatari and the Sforza. It is between the Balderdash and the Sforza."

"The Balderdash! Are you telling me we're in alliance with the Balderdash?"

"Yes, Sir. I'm afraid we are."

"So the princess made it all up? But how could she have known the contract number?"

"She is listed in the contract, Commander. But as an enemy, both of the Balderdash, and, since the signing of the contract, us."

Sal paced up and down. His brow was furrowed. "I don't want the Balderdash as my allies!"

"That is what the Count has agreed to."

"I choose my own enemies!"

"Forgive me, sir, but as a paid employee of the

Sforza, it is more correct to say the Count chooses them for you."

"I don't like it," Sal muttered, slumping into a chair. "And if I don't like it, I don't have to do it."

"You will have Count Sforza himself as your enemy if you persist in this course. What is the matter if I may ask? Count Sforza has been very good to you."

"Picking me was a good deal for him." Sal responded, "I was a Senior Pinball Wizard the year of my graduation, one of the best sixteen-year-old prospects to come along in a decade. That's what the newspapers said. He was lucky to get me."

"Perhaps so. But he has done well by you. It isn't every young man of sixteen who gets appointed bubaldar after only one year of service."

"It's just bubaldar second-class, the lowest rank that can hold independent command."

"Didn't he appoint you Sackmeister of Aldoona when your forces overran the Sachaverell Salient?"

"Sure, he made me Sackmeister," Sal said. "But what about Jacopo Kelly? He made him a zumdwiller third-class, and he hadn't even fought in a campaign!"

"Give the count time. He'll see to your advancement. But do not attempt to go against his wishes by attempting to put the princess on the throne of Melchior."

"Hell," Sal said. "I've already promised her I'd do that."

"That was before you knew she'd lied to you."

"Yes, that's so. Well, I guess we'll have to tell her."

"We, Commander?

"I know, I have to tell her myself. Is that it?"

"That's proper form," Toma said.

"Damn it, it's awkward…."

Just then the alarm went off.

"It's the men returning!" Sal said. "Thanks for the Oreos, I have to get back to the Command Room."

CHAPTER FIVE

The StarSwarm of Sal's Battle Group made a brave spectacle as they returned to the Battleship *Endymion* in their small, sleek spaceships. They came in fast from outer space, driving toward the *Endymion* at full bore, keeping up their speed until the last possible moment, then making a short, sizzling, braking turn just before they would have crashed into the big ship's hull. Sal had warned them over and over not to do that because there was always the possibility of a mistake, and he was responsible to Sforza Management Services if any of his craft were dented or destroyed. But the men were unable to resist the dashing gesture. Although they were full grown, they had signed with the Sforza Condottieri for the fun of it as well as for the money. They had all taken the Immaturity Option which let them have childish enjoyment in simple things. Sometimes Sal envied them. But he had chosen a different path, giving up much of his own enjoyment in order to get ahead. There'd be plenty of time for him to relax and play the fool when he was older. Right now, he needed to make his way in the world. Fun would have to come later.

Sal's second-in-command, Dick Fogarty, reported on the success of the campaign. He was a big man in his late twenties, already balding, hearty and thick of chest, and with a scruffy blond beard.

"Hi there, Commander!" Fogarty cried as he stepped into the Command Room.

"Welcome back, Soldier," Salvatore said. "How did the battle go?"

Fogarty told him how their StarSwarm had crept into Ratisbone, the enemy stronghold at Star Pass Nine, and descended into the planet's atmosphere unnoticed through their skilful use of the high-beam deflectors that gave their descent a virtual invisibility.

The StarSwarm had gone down through the clouds, coming out at last, twenty ships strong, over the city of Aria. They had caught the enemy completely by surprise.

And then the destruction began. The Ratisbone air militia scrambled to get space-borne, and were destroyed piecemeal by Fogarty's wing-men. The lamentations were loud from Ratisbonean mothers grieving for their fighter-spaceship sons and husbands who had tried, too late, to get aloft.

After a brief battle, Fogarty's men isolated the main city of Aria with volleys of lava fall, creating a fiery barrier between the city and the garrison of Space cadets who were pledged to defend it. The ships of the Sforza Condottieri had gone into their berserk dives, their jets burning fiery trails at oblique angles across city streets. Rain clouds exploded into sweaty evaporation as they dived beneath them, maximum-g burning, and came up with guns blazing.

They could have used the nuclears, of course, but that was frowned upon. Ever since the old days when atomics had nearly wiped out civilization, this form of warfare had been held in disrepute. The Universal Gaming Board, which controlled all combat setups, had set down stringent rules, working on a complex scale of war game simulation packages in hopes of someday weaning mankind from its favorite pursuit of unlimited destruction.

"To sum up, Sir, we destroyed the place, and I believe we did you proud," Fogarty said.

"I'm glad to hear that," Sal said. "I expected no less. I suppose all the men behaved properly?"

Dick Fogarty frowned and turned away. "Yes sir. All except Carruthers, who turned tail and ran when the first enemy resistance was encountered."

Salvatore scowled. "I'll not have cowardice in my Corps!"

"We know that, Sir," Dick said. "We took the liberty of following Carruthers when he tried to take refuge on one of the East Range Planets."

"What did you do to him?" Salvatore asked.

Fogarty drew a finger across his throat and rolled his eyes.

"Mercifully, I hope?" Sal said.

"After the first moment, he didn't feel a thing," Fogarty said.

"You've all done well."

Just then Toma hurried in.

"Announcing the arrival of the Princess Hatari," he said.

"What's she doing back here already?" Sal asked.

"You invited her to dinner."

"I didn't say when, though, did I?"

"You told her to come over after the squadron returned. She must have watched them from her ship's viewport."

"She seems to be in a great hurry?" Sal asked.

"Perhaps she's hungry," Toma said.

Dick Fogarty had followed this conversation with a puzzled look on his face.

"Do we have a visitor, Sir?" he asked. "I did notice a new ship parked near the dorsal fin when we came in."

"Her name is Princess Hatari," Sal said. "I've invited her over to dinner. See that the chaps get cleaned up as quickly as they can, all right?"

"Yes. sir! Is she pretty, sir?"

"Pretty troublesome," Sal muttered.

"Beg pardon, sir?"

"Never mind. Just tell everyone to get ready. Dress uniforms."

Dick Fogarty saluted and left.

"What are you going to do, sir?" Toma asked.

Sal said, "I'll tell her that we're enemies after dinner."

CHAPTER SIX

Sal asked the princess to wait for half an hour while Dick Fogarty detailed a group of men to act as caterers' assistants. They found plans for a party in an old manual. The men went to work at once, hanging bunting up on the walls, gluing paper emblems into prominent positions, waxing the floors and replacing dead light bulbs from the big overhead electric candelabra in the Officers' mess. Suitable music was found in the ship's library: baroque pieces which lent the air of stately procession that the military loves so much, as well as military two steps, and marches for tuba and trumpet.

Sal supervised it all. It was important to him to get this right.

The officers wore their best uniforms for the occasion. In their neatly pressed whites, with military caps pulled over their eyes at a rakish angle, they looked the very soul of the military establishment.

The autocook was reprogrammed to Banquet Mode. It took a few minutes for it to get used to the change, so long had it been doling out GI rations based upon Spam and rehydrated mock chicken. Now, however, the finest and most exquisite of foodstuffs were taken from ship's stores, defrosted and reconstituted with loving attention.

At the appointed time, the mess hall was brilliantly lighted with real candles set upon the sideboards. The long table was set with an immaculate white table cloth. The settings were laid with the squadron's finest china and silverware, taken out of storage for this gala occasion.

The room had been hastily re-paneled in genuine redwood shingles, part of the booty taken from the sacking of Oregonia, Planet of the Big Trees.

Salvatore sat at the head of the table, resplendent in the red and purple uniform of a bubaldar second-class in the Sforza Condottieri. His second-in-command, sometimes known as Dirty Dick, was cleanly shaven for a change. He sat at Salvatore's left hand. The place of honor on his right was reserved for Princess Hatari.

The officers talked quietly among themselves. They were not allowed to drink until the guest of honor had arrived, but they were permitted to smoke.

Ever since the invention of the artificial lung replacement operation in 2307 by Doctors Baxter and Cough, cigarettes had regained their previous role as chic indulgences. There was no reason now for anyone in the civilized galaxy not to smoke, since the lung replacement operation was simple and painless, involving no more than the sniffling of a tiny pill up a nostril, which, seated in the remnants of the tattered and blackened lung, would presently expand and exfoliate, like a growing sponge, dissolving old lung material and expanding until it occupied a predetermined mass.

A smart slap on the back was sufficient to start the new lungs working. If no one was around to perform the requisite back-slap, one could thump oneself on the chest with a patent chest-starter supplied free of charge. The new lungs worked even better than the original models, and it was often wondered why mankind had not thought of this centuries ago, rather than forego the pleasures and benefits of smoking.

R. J. Reynolds the 25th, present President of the Universal Humanoids Assembly, and a direct clone of his famous tobacconic ancestor, had endorsed the product himself. Non-smokers were looked down upon as "not quite men, if you know what I mean." Even Sal smoked, though at sixteen, he was still on his original set of lungs.

The princess made her appearance, to a round of applause from the officers. She was clad in a white ballgown that embraced her splendid figure with a tactility that could not be overlooked. She had little fire opals in her ears, and a necklace of emeralds around her neck. Brilliant as her jewelry was, her eyes, which ranged in color from amethyst to sapphire depending on the lighting, outglittered them all. She seemed a symbol of all that was finest in the ancient art of planetary rulership, and the officers applauded as she took her seat on Sal's left

"Princess," Sal said, "you are most welcome to our

battleship. Allow me to introduce my officers."

Introductions were made and duly acknowledged by the princess. At last they could turn to the real purpose of the evening: eating, and, above all, drinking.

"Allow me to serve you a portion of this duck aspic," Sal said. He could be gracious, this teenage leader of the Sforza StarSwarm in the Semiramis region.

"You are most kind," Hatari said. "And what is that beige-colored dish with the complicated lid at the far end of the table?"

"That is a gruel of stewed peacock tongues," Sal said, "lightly seasoned with marjoram, vermillion and censta, and mixed with a base of carrot and lilies. But permit me also to serve you this dish of baby Belgian beets stuffed with tiny bifurcated breadfruits, a specialty of the island stars of the far Outreach."

"How courteous you are!" exclaimed the princess. "I could only wish that you were a man several years my senior, because we could then get together and enjoy those pleasures which hitherto I have enjoyed only in the pages of sleazy novels and ancient soap opera tapes."

"Princess," said Sal, "that is a good and courteous declaration on your part. Perhaps we can discuss it further at a later time."

"Perhaps we can," the princess said. "I will have Kukri remind me, since a princess cannot be expected to remember everything."

"And who, pray tell, is Kukri?"

"He is my companion, servant, and banker," the

Princess said.

"Of what race is he, if I may enquire?"

"He is a member of a race also called Kukri."

"Forgive my denseness, Princess," Sal said, "but is he perchance of an invisible race? For I have not seen him here at this banquet."

The princess laughed, a mellifluous sound. "He is still in my spaceship, recuperating from his hibernation. I have sent a message to him in Hibernation Mode, requesting his presence, and he has signified through modem that as soon as he comes out of his petrified yet necessary sleep, he will be happy to join us."

"That is good news indeed," Sal said. "Allow me to present my second-in-command, Dick Fogarty. And this many-tentacled creature here on my lap is Toma, a spider-robot, perhaps my best friend here in Space as well as my humble servant."

Toma folded his two topmost tentacles in a hieratic gesture. Fogarty said, "Pleased to meetcha, Princess. The presence of a lady queen or princess looks fine indeed in our humble mess hall."

"How genteel," the princess said, fluttering her eyelashes.

Just then there was a knock at the space-lock.

"That would be Kukri," Princess Hatari said.

Sal made a gesture, and two giant regimental Nubians, especially unfrozen and revivified for this occasion, tall dark men with gorgeous many-colored turbans, unlocked the hatch and threw open the great circular door. Standing in the doorway was a small creature about the size of a badger. He had an otter's whiskers, and pointed ears like a wire-haired terrier. He wore a red plaid coat which, open at either end, allowed his head and bushy tail to protrude. Animal-like he may have been, but a lively intelligence shone in his brown eyes and each paw had three fingers. Over the coat, he wore a green and silver cloak with high collar, breeches, and a small gray felt cap that might have been of sentimental value to him, since it afforded him little in terms of spectacularity.

"Hello," he said, "I'm Kukri of the Kukris."

"You are the princess' banker, I believe?" Sal said.

"And her friend, too, I would like to believe."

"Come, take your seat here at the table." Sal turned to the bodyguard standing behind him with drawn laser rifle. "Put that down for a moment and fetch an omni-species adjustable chair for Kukri."

The chair, a superAmes with fourteen adjustable posture-planes and twenty-three degrees of softness, was quickly produced.

"This will do nicely," Kukri said. He pattered across the room on all fours and jumped up to the chair, which was positioned between Hatari and Sal.

"Tell me, Princess," said Dick Fogarty, "if you have already been appointed to a planet, what do you need with a banker?"

The Princess laughed—a sound like tubular bells, only somewhat higher in pitch.

"I can see, Sir, that you know not the ways of royalty. We are supposed, when we come to a new planet, to throw a party for all the inhabitants. That costs a pretty penny. And although we get it all back in taxes, it must be paid for at the time. As you probably know, Universal Caterers accept nothing but solid money of a kind that can be traded easily on any interstellar exchange, market or bourse. So it was incumbent upon me to find a means of financing the aforesaid feast in order not to bring shame upon my home planet of Excelsus, and my ancestors, whoever they might be."

"That makes sense," Sal said.

"I'm glad you think so," Hatari said.

"Tell us, Princess," Sal said, "how did you come to lose this world we are to get back for you?"

"I have always wanted to own my own planet," she told Sal and his officers, simulated fire from the simulated wood fireplace making her eyes sparkle. "There's just something about it, having a whole world all to yourself. So when Mr. Kukri here offered to finance my obligatory coming-out party, I jumped at the chance."

Mr. Kukri said, in a squeaky high-pitched and slightly pompous voice, "On my planet we do not say 'jumped at the chance.' We say 'speeded into the mouth of opportunity.'"

"How interesting," Sal said, with a frown.

"Thank you," the Kukri said, secure in the self importance that imbues many badger-like creatures. "Yes, I was happy to finance the princess in her endeavor. And there's something my race gains by it, too."

"Indeed?" said Sal.

"By the terms of my deal with the princess, we gain

a home. Know, gentle Sir, we Kukri had been searching for a planet of our own for quite some time. It was tragic how we lost our own, but that is another story. You see, as you may have noticed, we are nonhumans, so from the princess' point of view, it would be as if we were not there. That makes it possible for her to share a planet with us without actually sharing one, if you know what I mean."

The Princess said, "So Kukri advanced me the money for the party and a few other things, like a throne, and I signed the papers and got title to Melchior and was just preparing to move in when I learned that, between the time of my acceptance of the offer and my actual arrival, a tribe of Balderdash had moved in and thrown things into an uproar."

"Couldn't you have them served with papers?" Sal asked. "I thought there were agencies of the Universal Ruling Board who took care of matters like this."

"Naturally, we applied to the proper authorities," Hatari said. "But you know what it's like in the bureaucracy."

"I understand the situation a little better now," Sal said.

"Are you going to help us?"

"Perhaps we could discuss that after the banquet."

CHAPTER SEVEN

After the banquet, the badger-like Kukri tapped at the door to Sal's stateroom.

"The door's unlocked," Sal called out.

Kukri entered. "You sent for me, sir?"

"You are Princess Hatari's banker, is that correct?"

"Yes, sir, it is."

"You paid her a considerable sum to allow your race to share the planet Melchior with her."

"Yes sir, we did. I signed the agreement myself. I had to find a home for my people."

Sal said, "I see by my atlas that Melchior is four fifths water. Were you disappointed when you discovered there was little land?"

"Not at all. We Kukris plan to evolve quite soon into a water-breathing species."

"Why should you want Melchior so badly?"

"It is a planet whose atmosphere fits our needs just as it is. We can't afford to replace the air."

He went on to explain that the Kukri race had been having many troubles in recent years. Once, they were quite a respectable species. They got along well with everyone. Then it was noticed that they had no opposable thumbs. Since intelligent races were always known to have opposable thumbs, the Kukris were downgraded to "intelligent animals" and their credit rating was irreparably damaged. Nobody wanted to trust an unintelligent species, not even though they were a race that held sing-songs involving millions of participants. That was considered interesting instinctive behavior, but hardly worthy of being called intelligent.

The trouble was, the Kukri weren't very ingenious mechanically, and this put them at a disadvantage against all of the other intelligent species. They could talk up a storm, but they couldn't even open a can with a standard can opener, much less drive a screw with a screwdriver or do anything that required the use of an opposable thumb.

There were two types of opposable thumbs available those days in prosthetic device form. One was purely decorative, looked just like a genuine opposable thumb, and was rather more imposing than many of that ilk. But it couldn't move. It was a model of a thumb rather than a working thumb in itself.

Those who could afford it bought the other device, a genuine opposable thumb. This thumb could not only touch all the fingers of the hand without assistance from the other hand, but also could bend at various angles of 360 degrees due to its ingenious ball-and-socket jointure.

Those who had these thumbs were even more dexterous than those born with natural opposability. The thumbs were constructed so, during sleep, the opposability feature could be turned off, in order to store up energy for the next round of use. This gave them advantages over other races with the old-fashioned natural kind.

"So you see, Sir," Kukri said, "the gaining of this planet means everything to us. We have nothing left to sell. Our own planet, Kukriphipolis, has no resources left. We sold them off years ago. Even our crops have been sold far into the future, to the Grumphul Debt Collectors who put them to uses too esoteric to mention. In fact, we Kukris are planning to slink off in the night, all of us, and move lock-stock-and-barrel to the new planet. We need to avoid the bailiff who will strip us of our life support systems."

"But if it's mostly water," Sal said, "what will you do? You're not amphibious yet."

"Not yet. We have already invested heavily in prefabricated underwater cities by scraping together the last wealth our planet afforded us: the last big trees, the semi-precious ores, the trash fish, the varmints canned for dog food, everything we could put together. We made a bargain with the princess, and I was sent along to make sure the terms were carried out."

"I'm afraid you've gotten yourselves into one hell of a mess," Sal said.

"Looks that way," Kukri agreed morosely.

"You must have known her claim to a Sforza contract was invalid. "

"I suppose I did, sir."

"Your people really haven't behaved very intelligently in this."

"I suppose not. But will you get our planet back for us?"

"I had better discuss that directly with the princess." Sal said.

CHAPTER EIGHT

When Sal and Toma were alone with Princess Hatari in the gloomy reception room just behind the mess hall, the young commander lost no time getting right to the point.

"Princess, you haven't been playing fair with me."

"Why do you say that?" she said evasively.

"You lied to me, for one thing. I've looked over that contract you cited. I don't see your name as one of the contracting parties."

"You checked up on me, huh?" the princess said, walking into the room and haughtily seating herself near the TV console.

"Your name doesn't appear as a signatory to the contract you cited. What's the story, Miss Princess, and, for that matter, what place are you a princess to? I mean, one doesn't meet princesses every day."

"Especially if one is only sixteen years old," the princess said with a little bite to her voice. "But know, young man, that I am a born princess of the planet Fulvia Liviana."

Salvatore turned to the robot. "That strikes a bell, though I can't think why. Ever hear of the place?"

"Of course," the robot said. "It's the mail-order royalty planet out near Archimedes, where you can send in a few hundred credits and get a parchment giving you a title and even a bit of land to go with it."

"Oh, this is outrageous!" the princess said. "Am I to have my royal credentials questioned by a weird octopus and a young squirt who thinks he's hot stuff because he commands a battleship?"

"This young squirt saved your life," Sal said quietly. "Of course, you may prefer to return to your spaceship and go away. The Balderdash are probably lurking nearby."

"I'm sorry," Hatari said. "I just hate being asked questions in an intimidating manner. You have rather a stern way about you, you know. Attractive, but stern."

"So I have been told," Sal said.

"I'm sorry I called you a squirt. And I apologize to you, Toma."

"Actually," Toma said, "we consider it a compliment to be likened to octopi."

Sal said, "Let's get back to business. Princess Hatari, you have not properly identified yourself as a Sforza client."

"But I gave you the contract number!"

"Your name is not on it as a contracting party."

"It's not? It must have been an oversight."

"Hardly. You are mentioned in the contract, but as the Enemy."

"Me? An Enemy?"

"Yes, an Enemy of the Balderdash, whom the Sforza

signed that agreement with. The Balderdash employed the Sforza Condottieri to take up arms against you."

"Maybe they did. But that doesn't make it right."

Salvatore laughed. "Princess Hatari, you have practiced a deception on me. You are not in alliance with the Sforzas, as you claimed. Quite the contrary, they are in alliance against you."

Hatari looked prepared to argue the point. Then she shrugged and smiled quite charmingly. "Well, I had to do something. The question is now, what are you going to do?"

"I'll have to think about it," Sal said.

CHAPTER NINE

"You should have told her it was no dice," Toma said later when he and Sal were alone. "You know you can't help her."

"I know. I just thought I could find an escape clause in the contract."

Sal put down the copy of it he'd had faxed from Central Universal Faxing. "But there's just no doubt. She's named as the Enemy. I have discretion in a lot of things, but not in this."

"Then you'll just have to tell her," Toma said.

"All right, I know," Sal said wearily. "Please call up the princess and tell her we'll be right over. We have something urgent we must discuss with her."

"We, sir?"

"What's the matter? Is there any reason you shouldn't come along?"

"I was right in the middle of provision inventory."

"It can wait," Sal said. He looked at Toma. The robot spider's sidemost tentacles were drooping, and had turned from their normal healthy purple-red to a sickly green. Sal remembered that spider robots were extremely prone to melancholia, brought on by embarrassing double binds.

"Oh, stay here," Sal said. "I'll do it myself."

CHAPTER TEN

Sal put on his lightweight spacesuit and went to see the princess on her ship.

Onboard, he was greeted by Kukri.

"Greetings, Commander. You are most welcome."

"I've come to see the princess. Where is she?"

Sal walked down the dusty corridors of the ship behind Kukri. He noticed the ship was an old Edison Explorer. The princess evidently could not afford anything better. There were original manufacturer's marks on the cross-members, and on the tired old turbines. It occurred to him that the princess was really out on a limb.

The storeroom was large and piled with equipment and baggage. On one side, a space had been cleared where the princess's throne had been set up. It was a proper-looking throne, large and high-backed, covered in plush, with gargoyles carved into its arms.

The princess was sitting forlornly on the throne. She was wearing a green robe of office and had a little coronet on her head. Despite her twenty-eight years she looked like a very unhappy little girl.

"We always take our own thrones," she told Sal.

"But I'll never get to use mine for real, will I?"

"I don't know," Sal said. "Perhaps you can find some other place to rule. Go back to Excelsus, Princess. They will find another planet for you to rule."

"Oh, you just don't understand."

"What is there to understand?"

The princess leaned forward earnestly.

"We get just one chance. There are new generations of ruler material on Excelsus always pushing behind us. We get a shot at one job. If we blow it, that's it."

"What happens then? They won't jail you, will they?"

"No. There's no punishment for failure to occupy a throne. But they'll never use me again. My breeding and conditioning will go to waste. My internal programs will go haywire without people to rule. I can be sure to age rather quickly. And I'll gain weight, the one thing I can't afford to do."

"But what will you do? Where will you go?"

"I'll need to find some quiet planet where I can be a bag lady. It's the standard other alternative for failed royalty. I hear that Earth has such positions open."

His heart went out to her.

"Take it easy, Princess. Of course I'm going to help you."

"But you can't! The Sforza contract...."

"It won't be the first time a Condottieri has made his own arrangements on the field of battle."

"But what will Sforza do to you?"

"Don't worry, I can handle him."

But of course that was a lie. He couldn't handle Sforza at all. But he couldn't turn the princess out to be a bag lady.

CHAPTER ELEVEN

Salvatore explained to Dick Fogarty, his second-in command, that he had decided to help Princess Hatari occupy the throne of Melchior.

"The men won't like it, Sir," Fogarty said.

"Since when," Salvatore asked, "do we care what the men like? They're paid to fight, not to pass moral judgments."

"The moral part doesn't concern them at all, Sir. The fact is, we work for Sforza and Sforza has a contract with the Balderdash."

"I gave my word to assist the princess before I knew of the contract."

"So?"

"So that means I can, in all fairness, support her side"

"But why would you want to? When Count Sforza hears about this, he'll have your hide."

"Let me worry about that."

"It could mean our necks, too."

"Not if you follow the orders of your superior officer, who happens to be me."

"Sir, why are you doing this?"

"I have my reasons," Salvatore said. He wasn't going to tell an ape like Fogarty about his boast to Alfonso, or about his own displeasure at still being a mere bubaldar at the age of sixteen. In fact, he was almost seventeen. That was long enough to hold inferior rank!

"The Count will thank me for this in the end," Sal said.

"I don't know," Fogarty said. "It ain't regular."

"I'll let you despoil the Balderdash baggage ships if you continue to follow my orders."

"Hmm," Fogarty thought it over. "Are the Balderdash very rich?"

"Fabulously wealthy, it is said," Sal said, hoping it was true.

"And we keep it all? No nonsense about rules of war?"

"The rules of this war are," Sal said, "winner takes all. That's us. We must give the Count his third, there can be no doubt of that. But the rest is for you and the lads."

"There's money in a bit of rebellion, eh, sir?" said Dick.

"More than you'll see otherwise."

"We'll follow you to hell and back for money," Fogarty said. "To a mercenary, money is like religion."

"I'll see that the worship is good," Sal said. "Tell the men of the StarSwarm to prepare for a departure to Melchior within the hour. Tell the navigator to plan a course for us that is well clear of black holes. We don't want to come out on the other side of Polaris. Set a

Grade One Alert. And do it quick, mister!"

"Aye, Sir!" Dick Fogarty said, overawed by the sudden cold precision of his small commander.

§

Soon thereafter, the fleet set sail for the attack on Melchior. The men cheered up at the prospect of fighting. They weren't too upset about fighting against the orders of their employer and indenture holder, Count Sforza. Nobody likes a boss, especially when he practices parasitism upon bodies bought in the Rough Slave Market, as was the rumor concerning Sforza. There wasn't a law against it, but it still made one feel sort of strange inside, working for a man like that. And anyhow, a good mercenary soldier was supposed to revolt against his own leaders from time to time. It was like a law of nature.

And so the battleship *Endymion* set sail with its StarSwarm of smaller ships strapped down to its external vanes: the deadly Mini dreadnaughts; the quick-darting Truculents; and the shifty, unpredictable Neerdowells.

CHAPTER TWELVE

The battleship *Endymion* was moving along toward Melchior, eating up the light-minutes and hours as it came to flank speed. The ship was already rigged for combat; repulsion screens were up and running, torpedo tubes were filled, and the long-distance radar pinged monotonously as the ship continued to accelerate through the close-packed stars that made up this region of Semiramis.

The *Endymion*'s crew had not been put on full alert yet. The special troops who were to do the actual ground fighting—two regiments of the Second Sofia Infantry Brigade—were still in the refrigerated hold, motionless in their frozen slumber. Sal knew enough not to revive them too soon; combat troops were apt to rebel unless there was a fighting situation immediately before them.

The princess remained aboard her own ship, which, secured to the *Endymion*'s hull, was coming along for the ride.

Sal had asked Toma to search out whatever he could about the Balderdash. The little spider robot worked at the computer for a while, then reported to the captain.

"So what have you found out about the Balderdash?" Sal asked.

"There are some mysteries about them," Toma replied. "First mention I could find in the databases was when the Martin-Harris Expedition found them living a poverty-stricken life on Unk, one of the moons of Thoris Major. Unk was a small dark place, and at that time, the Balderdash were very primitive. They didn't even possess reliable spaceships, since the solution to the O-ring problem of their antiquated propulsion systems had always eluded them."

"What are O-rings?" Sal asked. "Do we have them?"

"No, we have moved far beyond that primitive technology. Our ships utilize W-rings, and we expect to move soon to X-rings. But these were not known back then."

"Go on," Sal said. "What was it about the O-rings?"

"They were always failing," Toma said. "Consequently, the Balderdash ships didn't dare go very far. When Martin questioned them about their lifestyle and beliefs, the answers they gave were so preposterous, so unlikely, so off the wall, so ill-thought out and poorly considered, so downright foolish, blockheaded and just plain wrong-minded, that Martin's comment, at the end of his report, was a hastily scrawled 'Balderdash!' The commentators back at the Institute took that for their real name, and so it stuck."

"The expedition must have gotten the answers to some major questions about them," Sal guessed.

"Yes, but it left a few mysteries unanswered."

"Such as?"

"Well, for one thing, no one has ever seen them eating. It has been guessed that they do this in so messy a way as to gross out even themselves. For another they give signs of being partly plant in their physical makeup, sprouting leaves at certain times of year and then giving birth to certain monstrous fruit. This led to the thought that, unique among intelligent beings, they powered themselves through photosynthesis. But this was by no means certain."

"But what does that mean?" Sal asked.

Toma shook his head. "Our scientists still have not decided. When, some years later, another expedition visited them, they found that the Balderdash had solved their O-ring problems and gone on to build quite respectable spaceships of considerable speed, using the Owens-Watkins Bilateral Sub-space Drive though they never paid patent fees for it. In a very short time they had become a fighting race, though not of a sort that is generally respected.

"The Balderdash were cunning in battle, pretending to flee, then racing back to the attack in what was meant as a surprise move. Later they changed tactics when they found this surprised no one. Their ships were armed with long-range cannon and modified plasma torpedoes. They were known to be cruel, taking apart prisoners to see what made them tick and then putting them back together again in ingenious but shocking ways."

"Not nice people at all," Sal said. "Do they still live

on Unk?"

Toma waved his tentacles in an emphatic negative gesture. "They destroyed Unk in a nuclear accident after stripping it of any minerals of value. They have been looking for a new homeland ever since. But nobody wants them for neighbors. They are slovenly, and leave a mess wherever they go. Also they are ugly, especially with their intricately folded mouths."

"Just like the Kukris," Sal said. "They also are missing a planet."

Just then Dirty Dick Fogarty hurried into the room. "Commander! We have picked up a StarSwarm of armed ships just within radar range."

"See if you can raise them on radio," Sal said. Fogarty adjusted the radio, his hairy fingers surprisingly delicate on the luminous dials. "They're on Channel 2a22, Sir."

Sal turned to the channel and switched it on.

"Hello," a voice on the radio said, in Intergab. "Is anyone there?"

"Who's that?" Sal said. "Identify yourself, please"

"I am Selfridge Summum Lorn, commander of this Space Armada of the Balderdash."

"What do you want?" Sal asked him. "I hope you're not planning to try to stop me from going to Melchior."

"I had no such thought!" the commander said. "This battleship of yours. Is plenty big, no?"

"Damn right, it's big," Sal said.

"With many weapons, some of newfangled designs?"

"We're armed, and we're coming through."

"Okay," the Balderdash said. "Don't get sore. We got no complaints. We're not here to cause trouble. We're just here to make sure things go okay. In fact, we have a present for you."

A midshipman hurried into the Command Room.

"Small rocket-propelled object on the port bow, sir!"

"Scan it for explosive potential," Sal said.

The midshipman hurried to a phone and spoke briskly to the Materials Inspection Officer down in the Assay Office. He listened to the replay, then said, "It is inert, sir."

"All right. Bring it aboard."

The present from the Balderdash was a package about four feet to a side, wrapped in gaily colored paper. "Can we unwrap it, sir?" the midshipman asked.

"I suppose so," Sal said.

Swiftly they unwrapped the paper, folding it carefully back on itself, in the prescribed military manner for opening strange gifts. Beneath was a large box.

Willing hands swiftly opened the box. From within, a cloud of yellowish smoke trickled out. Sal reached for the button that would activate the firefighting machinery, but the smoke soon ceased, and in its place, images danced in the lambent light of the ship's Command Room. The images solidified into images of women, young and beautiful, scantily clad, and doing a kind of dance. The rest of the crew had crowded into the Command Room, and they watched the gyrations with every sign of pleasure.

As they watched, Sal became aware of an odd and

not unpleasant smell that swiftly permeated the room. It was an odor he could not immediately identify. Images sprang up to his mind, of spring days, sunsets, waves dancing on a sunlit sea, of love and remembrance, and many other things.

"Sir, wake up!" Toma cried, tugging at Sal's arm.

Sal came swiftly out of his trance. The spider robot pointed at the position screen. Sure enough, there were dots of light moving across the battleship at increasing speed. A constant readout of symbols showed they were a StarSwarm of Balderdash ships, and they were coming in fast.

"They're attacking!" Sal cried. "Stations, everyone!"

He ordered the engines Emergency Full Ahead. The big ship, powered by new position reentry props and null-mode reactors, moved swiftly into position facing the oncoming smaller ships head-on.

The Balderdashi on the radio was saying, "We have some stuff here we'd like you to check out."

Sal's nose crinkled. "What's that?" he asked,

"What's what?" Dick Fogarty said, his head reeling.

"It's coming from that package!" Toma said. "They're pumping pheromones into our air supply system!"

"Neutralize the atmosphere!" Sal ordered. "And rig for attack!"

CHAPTER THIRTEEN

Now was the time that Salvatore proved his worth. Modem rules of warfare called for the commander to pay close attention to all his ships. His controls in the main ship allowed him to override any pilot's individual controls. Thus he could form and re-form his ships, hurling them into battle at crucial points; they could support each other when the odds were against them, or let up when it looked like an easy kill.

Sal snapped himself into the big command chair. His fingers moved lightly over the buttons and switches and dials set in the panel in front of him. Read-out screens ahead and on either side of him gave him constantly updated information on the changing position.

The Balderdash StarSwarm opened out into Formation B12, known as the Toothed Basket, and swept in toward the giant battleship…. This maneuver was designed to enfold Sforza forces and make them the nexus of combined firepower.

It looked like Sal had walked into a trap. But he had a trick or two up his sleeve. No sooner was the formation complete, and the Balderdash licking their lipless mouths, so to speak, seeing that they had the

Endymion trapped, than Sal pulled a hairpin retro-reversal. It was a very difficult maneuver. Instant timing was called for. Most space battleships couldn't be trusted to execute so intricate a maneuver with any hope of success. And to make matters worse, the Balderdash StarSwarm had been joined by two other StarSwarms from bases on nearby planets, Dexter II and Port St. Planet. Their combined forces made them several times more capable than the *Endymion* and its StarSwarm, and with a combined weight of firepower capable of splitting whole planets asunder. Sal held his position and waited for the crucial moment. His fingers rested lightly on the switches and toggles. With his feet he was able to maneuver the side-bands, and he used his forehead for striking the firing node.

From the Balderdash viewpoint, it was as if the Battle Group suddenly disappeared from their sight. Not even radar could find them. Sal had performed a simultaneous sideways slip into another dimension.

He brought the ship out in null space, still maintaining control. Odd-shaped objects the size of moonlets floated nearby. It would be instant destruction if the ship were to touch them, because they were planets, shrunken down in the strangeness of null space but still in full possession of their mass and coriolis forces.

Sal maneuvered for a moment, avoiding the sudden static force lines from a nearby gray hole, and then brought the *Endymion* back into normal Space. He came out exactly where he had planned, behind and above the alien StarSwarm, which was still splayed out in the now vulnerable basket maneuver.

"Now go get them, boys!" Sal cried, and turned control over to the individual ships of his own StarSwarm.

The men of the battle group didn't have to hear that twice. The squadron leaders were already aboard their ships, waiting for the Commander's signal. "Tallyho!" they cried, and their ships screamed away from the mother ship and bored into the Balderdash formation.

Plasma cannons flung red death. Gigantic tractor beams tore ships from the sky and battered them against a barren little comet that had wandered into the vicinity. Sparks flew in glittering arrays. Electrical potentials looped from ship to ship across the darkness of Space, now lit by the fire from exploding Balderdash ships. It was all over in a minute. The Balderdash beat a hasty retreat. Below the *Endymion* was the blue-green-white mass of the planet Melchior.

CHAPTER FOURTEEN

There was a large Balderdash military installation still in place on Melchior. They were situated in a fortress set into the largest land mass. Sal radioed to this fortress at once.

"I want to land on the planet," Sal said.

"No, you can't," the Balderdash commander radioed back. "This is our planet."

"This planet is not yours," Sal said. "Please clear out at once and there will be no further trouble."

"Not a chance," the Balderdash commander replied. "We found this planet and we intend to keep it. Go away and we will not have to destroy you and your Battle Group."

"That I have to see," Sal said. "Your armada tried to destroy *Endymion* and failed. I think it is you who should go away."

"We? Never!"

CHAPTER FIFTEEN

Endymion was set on Hover Mode five kilometers above the planet's surface. The landing parties were told to get ready. The men of the boarding parties were armed with spun-fire rifles and quick edge bayonets. They had grenades of great power and efficiency. And they were fighting mad.

Sal had the foresight to pass out quantities of Fury 12, the drug that makes fighters out of everyone. With fury beating in their brains, with rushes coursing up and down their venous systems, the men of the StarSwarm landed on the ground and fanned out into open position.

There wasn't much ground to cover on Melchior. But the Balderdash had access to the resources of the planet. They'd had the foresight to set up hastily fabricated underwater cities, and they retreated to these. From them, they set up a spirited resistance. Sal landed his men on one of the island land masses and set out to destroy the underwater city. This seemed straightforward enough. Underwater moles advanced, air bubbles bubbling from their discharge pipes. The men, now in underwater gear, prepared for a final assault on the city.

CHAPTER SIXTEEN

Space battles were the main event, but there was often a need for land battles, too. For this, special soldiers were imported from various planets with surplus populations. These soldiers were given a brief training course, it being essential for them to look good in front of the Universal Judges who oversaw land-based planetary contests.

These special soldiers were kept in storage until they were needed. The bunks were stacked one on top of the other, from wall to wall, and from floor to ceiling. There were narrow aisles in between, just wide enough for the clean-up crew. Every bunk was equipped with life-support and resuscitation equipment.

The soldiers lay comatose in their bunks, needles in their arms, oxygen masks on their faces, soft music playing, awaiting the call that bade them wake and rise.

§

The resuscitation alarm went off down the corridors of the hold. Glaring overhead lights came on and began to flash. Sirens and shrill whistles sounded. The life-support equipment increased its pace. Adrenalin fractions were poured into intravenous needles and plunged into supine arms.

The soldiers stirred, tossed and moaned, emitted loud grunts, scratched themselves, rubbed their eyes, shook their heads, saying, "Wha—? What's that?" They climbed out of their bunks. Folded under the mattresses were their uniforms, all neatly pressed. They slipped them on. They fell in, to the bellows of the newly-awakened drill sergeant.

Sal entered then. He called for silence, and then addressed his troops.

"Men, we are here today to say a few words for our comrades who will fall in the battle to come. There won't be many of them. Some of you lads are new, just arrived from the Soldier Factory. Those of you fresh from Lekk, pay special attention."

The men stood to attention when Salvatore rode onto the scene. His stirrups jiggled. His spurs flashed in the sunlight. He viewed his men with splendid disdain, but also with fatigue. He was tired. There had been many preparations to oversee.

CHAPTER SEVENTEEN

"Sir," Toma said, "there's a phone call for you."

"Can't you see I'm about to lead the men into a desperate action? Tell whoever it is I'll call back, if I survive."

"I think you'd better take this one," Toma said.

"Who do you have on the line?" asked Sal. "Sounds like it's God or something."

"More important, from your immediate point of view. It's Count Sforza."

"Rats!" Sal said.

§

"Sal? Is that you?"

"Yes, it's me, Count. Can you hear me?"

"Speak up, would you? I think we've got a bad connection."

"Let me turn up the Pattern Suppression Program. There, is that better?"

"Much better. Sal, what do you think you're doing?"

"I'm about to lead my men into battle," Sal said. "In fact, this is not the greatest moment for me to be chatting with you."

"Now you listen to me, young man. You're about to engage in a battle with the Balderdash, is that correct? What did you say? What was that word?"

"I said yes," said Sal sullenly.

"But has it not been explained to you that they are our allies?"

"So I've been told. But there's something ominous about these Balderdash. I really mean that, sir, I think we'd better go with the Princess."

"You think? Who told you that you could think?"

"I'm supposed to think," Sal said, "when I'm Senior Commander on station."

"Thinking is one thing," Sforza said. "Starting a war against an ally is another thing. Sal, break off this action at once."

"Damn!" Sal said.

"What is it?"

"The attack just began."

"But how could it begin? You didn't give the signal, did you? A battle can't start until the commander makes the signal."

"When you told me to break off the action," Sal said, "I got so upset, I pounded my right fist into the palm of my left hand."

"So?"

"That was also the gesture I'd selected for beginning the battle."

"Sal," Sforza said, with deadly quietness, "I want you to end this fighting immediately, apologize to the Balderdash, and come to see me. I think it's time we had a little talk."

"Yes, Sir, right away, Sir," Sal said.

CHAPTER EIGHTEEN

Salvatore was in a state of dejection. Here he was, so near to victory, and his warlord, Count Carmine Sforza, had ordered him to cease and desist, to hand over his hard-fought victory to the Balderdash and come home forthwith, if not sooner.

Despite orders, he had jet-chuted with his troops to the surface of Melchior. They had landed unopposed, and had formed a command post.

The princess, too, was dejected. She had come down to Sal's command post on Melchior by launch from the hovering battleship *Endymion* in order to be at hand for the victory celebration. She had worn her new coronation gown, which was emerald-green with diamonds. They were actually zircons, but she planned, after she had access to the treasury of Melchior, to replace them with real ones.

"One owes it to the people," she explained, "to show proper pomp and circumstance."

"You might as well forget about coronation gowns," Sal said. "We're in serious trouble here."

"But you can do something about it, can't you?" Hatari asked, in melting tones which were lost on the scowling sixteen-year-old.

"l don't know what I can or can't do," Sal said. "Let me think for a moment...."

He stood up and began pacing up and down the rough-hewn floor of his command post. The men moved to get out of his way. Sal was a good commander and well liked by his men, but he was known to have a temper. He scowled, twisting his mouth this way and that and squinting his eyes. He scuffed his feet as he walked. At last he walked up to a comer of the room, put his face close to the wall, and screamed in a high-pinched ululation that startled the princess exceedingly, but did not fluster the men, who were well accustomed to their commander's way of letting off steam.

Sal composed himself. "All right," he said, "where is the Land Communications Officer?"

"That's part of my job," Dick Fogarty said.

"This place has a native population."

"Yes, sir. The Simis, they're called."

"How far away is the nearest Simi town?"

"There's one just beyond the ridge there," Fogarty said.

Sal checked this out on the telescopic periscope. This instrument, with proper adjustment, brought the landscape into high focus. Sal looked out on a green and orange landscape, with brown earth tones here and there as accents. There were trees, though they didn't look like any that Sal had ever seen. They were like gigantic mushrooms, colored orange, and with feathery leaves of peacock green. There were ridges and fault lines in the land. Beyond the meadow that lay ahead of him, Sal could see what looked like a fair-sized town or small city.

Sal turned to Fogarty, "Do you think you could take a squad of men and bring me back an adult Simi?"

"Sure, Boss," Fogarty said. "If you're planning on torturing him, I'd better get a strong one."

"This is for questioning, not torturing," Sal said.

"Okay, Commander." Fogarty turned to select a few men. But suddenly a cry from the man on the furthest outpost guard was heard. "Sir! A sentient being is coming here!"

Sal looked through the periscope again. He saw a creature that looked like a kangaroo, except that it had bright green fur with scanty feathers. Vestigial wings flapped as it hopped along. Its skull was larger than that of a kangaroo, with the telltale bulge at the occipital lobes generally associated with intelligence.

"Saves us the trouble of going out and rounding him up," Sal said. "Check him for weapons and send him to me."

CHAPTER NINETEEN

On a signal from Sal, the guard opened the door of the command Post and allowed the Simi to enter. Up close, Sal could see that the creature's eyes were bright green, with a few dots of yellow. He didn't know if it meant anything or not.

"Do you speak Intergab?" Sal asked.

"Yes, among others," the Simi said, speaking in a clear, unaccented Intergab. "I am a translator, so I speak a number of off-world languages as well as our native tone, Ou'Simi."

"Welcome to my ship," Sal said. "I am a bubaldar in the Condottieri of Count Carmine Sforza. I have come here to set you free of the heavy hand of the Balderdash."

"You're going entirely too fast for me," the Simi said, blinking and squinting. "You're rather indistinct, too."

"Maybe you need glasses," Fogarty suggested, and began to guffaw until he was silenced by a glare from Salvatore.

"We can see perfectly well, but only when things are in their customary shape and colors." He squinted hard for a moment at Sal. "You're bipedal, aren't you? Two legs? Yes, I thought I spotted that. Now, what did you say you wanted?"

"I want to free you of the conquering Balderdash," Sal said.

"Who are they?" the Simi asked in a puzzled tone.

"Big, tall, skinny fellows with folded mouths," Sal said.

"Oh, yes! The Benefactors! That's what we call them."

"The Balderdash, benefactors? You must be thinking of some other race."

"No, the Balderdash are the only new arrivals here. They've come to help us, you know. We Simi are pitiable creatures, and much in need of help. The Balderdash have agreed to do all of the work that needs doing on this planet. That's quite a lot, you know."

"But you elected to have a queen," Sal said.

"Yes, but then the Balderdash came to talk to us, and we changed our minds."

"Perhaps you should reconsider. A queen would be very good for you. I've brought her along. You'll like her."

"We probably would like her," the Simi said. "We like most peoples and races and things. But she wouldn't do what the Balderdash are doing for us. They're doing all the work, man! They're even taking care of the egg factories in which we raise our young. That frees millions of us to do other things."

"But how can you just turn over your eggs to some alien race?" Sal asked.

"It's not so hard. I mean, they're just eggs. They just lie there, you know what I mean? The only interesting thing about an egg is the moment it breaks. And then it isn't an egg any longer. It's another mouth to feed."

"You don't like to take care of your own eggs? But all of you were eggs when you were young!"

"Sure, but that was back before we knew better. The Balderdash take care of the eggs now, and we do other more important stuff."

"Like what?"

"We walk in the great forests and look for blue leaves."

"Are they hard to find?"

"No, not particularly."

"Then why do you do it?"

The Simi looked at him, open-mouthed. "That doesn't sound like a friendly question. We just do it, that's all."

"How can you let aliens do all these things for you?"

"Low self-esteem," the Simi said. "We don't think much of ourselves. That's because we aren't very bright, and we aren't very warlike. But we do like to walk in the forest and collect blue leaves. It would be a better world if everyone did that."

"Do all of you feel this way?"

"Oh yes, all," the Simi said. "Every Simi feels the same as every other Simi feels. That way we avoid differing opinions."

CHAPTER TWENTY

"So now what?" Toma asked.

Sal shrugged. He was in his Command Post, a prefabricated structure, a tent actually, with rugs on the floor and lamps hanging from the cross members. There was a constant coming and going of armed men wearing the distinctive silver and purple livery of the Sforzas, and the fancy little caps with eagle feathers in them. There was a communication center by means of which Sal could keep in touch both with his men, who were strung out in squads, and with the spaceship, hovering high overhead. There was a smell of sweaty efficiency about the place.

The princess came in, looked at the sulky boy and the nervous spider robot. She sat down with a sigh and looked at Sal."You have tried, but they don't want me," she said. "Acknowledge your Count's order. I will go away."

"No," Sal said. "Not yet."

"What will you do?"

"Look," Sal said, "something is very wrong here. All our evidence shows the Balderdash are evil and cruel. Why would the Simi want them? What deception have they practiced on these unsophisticated folk?"

"We'll never know. There's no time to find out."

"We have to find out. I have to find out what the Balderdash are doing in the Simi cities."

"But there's no way for you to get through the Balderdash lines, to the main population centers."

"I can think of one possibility? He turned to Toma. "Call Alfonso on the special frequency."

CHAPTER TWENTY-ONE

"This is a crazy scheme," Alfonso said.

He had just arrived by his own ship from the mine shafts fifty miles away in Moronmsia Prefecture, where he had been studying the mineral profile of the planet. There had been hasty greetings. Sal had explained his dilemma, and Alfonso had agreed to help his zygote brother. Now, under cover of darkness, Alfonso was leading Sal and Toma across the no man's land toward the Simi city.

"I need to know exactly what is going on in there," Sal said.

"It's dangerous, going in there."

"It's the only way of resolving this," Sal said.

"We'd better get moving," said Toma.

They moved quickly through the darkness. Sal and Alfonso were wearing shapeless gray-brown sacks. This had been Alfonso's idea. Knowing how limited Simi vision was, he hoped that wearing these outfits on such a dark night would enable them to pass as natives.

The city gates were not locked. They went in, quickly, furtively. All was quiet inside except for the chatter of many TVs set up on poles. The Simi had a great fondness for TV and had bought many years' worth of *Fawlty Towers* reruns. They claimed the show was funny even from an alien viewpoint.

Sal, Alfonso and Toma proceeded down narrow deserted streets, the buildings bulging with dark quaintness on either side. They went through the main square, down a cobblestoned road into a clearing. And there across the street was a very large building made of red brick.

"This is the egg factory," Alfonso said.

The gate was secured with a massive chain and padlock, but the hasp on the padlock had not been locked into place. They swung open the gate and went in. The place was empty. The guards and workers were away.

"Where is everyone?" Sal whispered.

"Watching the midnight spear-fishing competition," Alfonso said.

"A break for us," said Sal.

"I hope so," Alfonso said. "I have to get back to the mines now. Good luck!"

After he departed, Sal and Toma entered the factory.

CHAPTER TWENTY-TWO

Inside the factory, there were rows of bassinets, temperature-controlled, under dim overhead lights.

Sal walked down one of the aisles between the rows of bassinets, where the eggs lay, three or four to a basket.

Sal recognized the Simi eggs, having previously looked them up in his Egg Identification Book. The Simi eggs were colored reddish-brown, about four inches long, pointed on one side, rounded on the other. But there was another kind of egg in the bassinets, too. These were slightly smaller, colored grayish white with purple specks. They were perfectly round in shape.

Now what were these eggs? Sal stared at the purple-specked eggs. There was something disturbing about them. He lifted one of them in one hand, and held a regular reddish-brown Simi egg in the other: The purplish eggs were heavier, and faintly greasy to the touch.

"These are not Simi eggs," he said to Toma.

The spider robot touched one of the purplish eggs with a delicate tentacle. "You are right, Sir. They do not appear to be Simi at all. But what are they'?"

"I think we know the answer to that," Sal said. "Did you bring the Egg Identification Book?"

"I have it right here," Toma said. He took the book out of the small day-pack he had strapped to the widest part of his frame. "Let's see now, purplish, perfectly round...." He flipped the pages quickly. "Here it is, Commander!"

There on page 44 was a perfect reproduction of the egg. Beneath it, the text read, "Reproduction of Balderdash egg."

"So!" said Sal.

"Yes, indeed," Toma said. "You have penetrated to the heart of the mystery, Sir."

"It's obvious enough now," Sal said. "The Balderdash have given all those good things to the Simi in order to have access to their egg factories. Once in charge, they have put their own eggs into the bassinets along with those of the Simi."

"And the purpose of that...?"

It came to Sal in a blinding flash of horrified insight.

"When the Balderdash fledglings hatch out, they will kill the Simi fledglings. Then the Balderdash will be able to take over all of Melchior and populate it with their own noisome spawn."

Toma curled one tentacle in a thoughtful gesture.

"Why didn't the Simi notice the different eggs."

"You know how hard of seeing they are. The Balderdash must have counted on that."

Toma nodded a tentacle. "We must report this to the proper authorities at once."

"There's no time," Sal said. "Listen." He held the Simi egg out to Toma.

The spider robot took the egg and turned it carefully in his tentacle. "What am I listening for, Sir?"

"Hold it to your ear," Sal said.

Toma did so. "Something inside is moving!" he exclaimed.

"Exactly the case. These creatures are within a few hours of hatching. Once they're out, it will be too late."

"What are we to do?" Toma asked.

Sal looked around. In a corner of the factory, he saw a barrel filled with brass stock. He took a piece about two feet long, heaved it, then strode purposefully to the nearest bassinet.

"I don't know if this is such a good idea," Toma said.

"Never mind what you think. Help me."

He bent over and tapped at one of the Balderdash eggs. He tapped a second time. He gave a third, firmer tap, and the egg began to fissure. Crazed lines appeared on its spherical surface. Then it split in two, and from its interior poked a bald, beaked face with a curiously folded mouth.

"Mon Dieu!" the robot exclaimed. "It is coming at me!"

The fledgling had bared its long teeth. Its little eyes flashed an angry red. It advanced on the spider robot, who backed away.

"Why is it pursuing me?" Toma asked.

"It is the nature of the Balderdash," Sal said. "In the Egg Identification Book, it says that the Balderdash are at their most ferocious just after birth. Some say it is their anger at having been born into a world of pain and baffled desire. But that is just a theory. It is certain that they attack anything that moves except each other."

"That is interesting," Toma said. "But isn't there anything you can do about this one? It is trying to eat one of my tentacles."

Sal pulled out his blaster, set it for narrow beam, and quickly converted the fledgling into smelly charcoal. Then he and Toma walked up and down the aisles of the egg factory, smashing and destroying the Balderdash eggs.

At last the task was done. "We've succeeded," Sal said. "These creatures will never breed out into an unprepared world."

"Amen to that," Toma said. "Now we must explain all this to Count Sforza."

CHAPTER TWENTY-THREE

Back in his camp, Sal sat alone in his two-story Command Post and pondered his next move, sipping the cup of Ovaltine that Toma had prepared for him.

He fell into a deep concentration. He came out of it only when he noticed a shadow crossing the room, and then a quiet sound behind him. Sal got quickly to his feet and turned. He saw three men coming down from the ceiling. They were dressed entirely in black, with most of their faces concealed in hoods. They had swords strapped across their backs. They had on light-weight super-adhesive sneakers which enabled them to walk right down the walls, though the strain on their back and hip joints was considerable. Moving with sinuous grace, they came to the floor and reset their suction cups. And then they were ready.

The three Ninja advanced shoulder to shoulder on their gray sneakered feet. They were all smiling, a sign that Sal found ominous. He glanced quickly to either side and saw that his accustomed weapons were out of reach. There was his ray sword, hanging from a peg on the wall. There was his blaster, its bulbous Lucite butt glowing with restored energies, just the weapon for cutting these suckers down. But it, too, was out of reach.

It occurred to Sal that he could perhaps sidle up to the blaster while diverting the Ninjas with conversation.

"Hi, fellows, what's happening'? he asked, skillfully feigning the manner and disingenuous gaze of an adolescent.

"We come to get you," the foremost Ninja said.

"Is that a fact?" said Sal. "And where do you want to take me?"

"Don't go sidling up to them weapons," the foremost Ninja said.

There was no time for delay. The blaster was almost within his reach, there in the suddenly stifling hot room, with the view of Melchior's double moons visible in the upper left-hand quadrant of the window.

Sal made his move, but it was too late. The Ninjas were all around him. There was a sharp rap behind his left ear. His vision exploded into light and jagged color, and that was all he remembered.

CHAPTER TWENTY-FOUR

Sal returned to consciousness with a pain in his head. He was lying on a cold stone floor in a room about ten feet square. There was just one window, high up on the wall. It was barred.

Sal got to his feet and paced up and down the room, regaining his energy, He realized that the gravity was lighter, and there was a freshness and tang to the air. He was no longer on Melchior.

There was a grating sound of a key in the lock. The door opened. A man in plain battle-dress, with a blaster in his hand, entered cautiously.

"You there! Come with me."

Sal asked him, "Where am I?"

Once in the corridor, the guard gestured. "Know you not the characteristic groined architecture of the imperial Palace of the Sforza on the planet Rienzi?"

"So I'm on Rienzi. I was afraid of that."

Count Sforza had him in his grasp! A thousand thoughts swept through Sal's mind. Could he over-power the guard and run? But where could he run to? Sforza had the power to pluck him from any planet, no matter how distant, and bring him here. He would not be safe anywhere.

Sal followed the guard down a long, dimly lit corridor, and then through a doorway to an interior courtyard. In niches along the walls, there were antique marble statues of stem-looking Roman types.

They entered a room where Sforza sat playing with toys. Sal remembered now how much Sforza loved new and complicated toys of all sorts. These new ones looked fascinating, all black and silver. Sal didn't know how they worked, but he longed to find out.

The Count put down his toy and turned to Sal. He was a big man, with a prominent belly partially concealed by his flowing ermine robe. His face was round, self-indulgent and a little cruel. He wore a small moustache and pointy beard.

"Sal, Sal," he said, "what am I to do with you?"

"Where'd you get the new toys?" Sal asked.

Sforza smiled. "You like them, don't you? They're the latest import from the Play Planet."

"I've never heard of the Play Planet before."

"It's just recently begun operation in the Delta Sigma system. Their motto is, 'A place for the young in heart and heavy in pocketbook.'"

"These look neat," Sal said.

"They are," Sforza said. "I have them here with me now so that you may know what you are going to miss. There'll be no toys where I'm sending you, my lad."

"Where's that?" Sal asked.

"You're going to the Dullsville Camp on Planet Trabajo. There you will pick lima beans with the slave peon robots and listen to self improving lectures every evening. You will not like it, Sal. It will be dull and tiring work, just the kind you hate. My heart goes out to you. But there's nothing I can do about it. You disobeyed my order, and you must be punished."

Sal shrugged and looked stoical. Sforza sighed and played with one of his new glittering toys. It made satisfying squeaks when he turned it one way and giggled when he turned it another.

"I could forgive almost anything else, Sal," Sforza said. "But why did you have to lose my spaceship?"

"What are you talking about? I left it parked in orbit when I went down to Melchior."

Sforza shook his head. "When my Ninjas grabbed you, the *Endymion* took off soon after, and has not been seen since. I assume you had left orders to that effect."

"I did not!"

"Of course you'd say that," Sforza said. "Whatever happened, you're responsible."

"Of course I am," Sal said. "If the ship's lost, I'll pay for it."

"Out of what? Your salary as a commander for the next thousand years wouldn't cover it. And you're not going to be on commander salary any longer."

Sal shrugged, "Then there's nothing I can do about it."

"You can tell me what you did with the ship. You must have left some kind of standing orders. You must know where they were going."

"I really don't have a clue," Sal said.

Sforza crossed the room and sat down on a low pedestal. "I should have listened to my advisors. They told me it was crazy to entrust a trillion dollar space-ship to a fourteen-year-old kid,"

"I'm sixteen!"

"But you were fourteen when I turned the ship over to you."

"You know yourself," Sal said, "that we teenagers have proven far more reliable than mature men like yourself."

"Don't you go getting smart with me, young man," Sforza said.

Sal hung his head, but peered up defiantly through his tousled red-orange curls. The freckles on his cheeks glowed like battle stars.

Sforza said, "I see that I am going to have to give you a taste of the agonies you will soon endure. I have prepared a documentary of the sorrows and discom-forts that await you on Trabajo."

"Why bother when I'll soon enough be enduring the real thing?"

"Because I want you to brood over what's going to happen to you on Trabajo before it actually happens."

"If that's a Renaissance subtlety, it's beyond me," Sal remarked.

Count Sforza glared at him. Fury colored his face and engorged his neck. It was a crucial moment for the two. The Condottieri ruler and his young commander were on the verge of saying words that would have wounded each of them to the quick and rendered impossible any chance of compromise. But at that moment, a guard ran into the room, his unbuttoned gorglet sign enough of his haste.

CHAPTER TWENTY-FIVE

"Sire!" the guard cried. "The battleship *Endymion* has just reappeared!"

The occupants of the room stared at each other in wild surmise, for at that moment the receptor plate of the Instantaneous Transfer Machine glowed. Three figures appeared in its field, shadowlike at first, then swiftly taking on substance. They were Alfonso, Toma, and Kukri.

Sforza's surprise quickly gave way to rage. "What did you do with my ship?" he thundered at the new arrivals.

"What any lover of mankind would have done," Toma said. The spider robot advanced to the center of the room. Fatigue was evident in his drooping central tentacles. But he held his spherical body proudly erect and said, "I took over the *Endymion* and followed the Balderdash when they fled from Melchior. This was soon after your Ninjas kidnapped Commander Sal, not long after he had destroyed the Balderdash eggs."

"Destroyed whose eggs?" said Sforza. "I was not told of this."

Sal explained how the Balderdash had been substituting their own eggs for the Simi eggs, obviously with the intent of killing off the entire new generation of Simis and replacing them with Balderdash.

Count Sforza mused for a moment. Then he said, "That was well done. And then you followed them?"

"Yes, Sire," said Toma. "To see where they would go."

"And where did they go?"

"I will let Kukri explain that," Toma said.

The badger-faced little alien stepped forward, cleared his throat, and said, "I know I am a mere under-species to you, and it is true that my race was born without an opposable thumb. Some have thought to heap defamy on us for that, contending that in the thinking department we are out to lunch, and other cruel metaphors of an inaccurate but compelling nature. And so—"

"Would you please get on with it?" Sforza said. "Before I have you stuffed?"

"Oh, sorry," Kukri said briskly. "I just wanted to explain that though unintelligent myself, nevertheless it seemed to me worthwhile to bring to your attention the Balderdash location. So that you could apply your own unquestioned intelligence to it, the intelligence which emanates from your possession of two opposable thumbs."

"Enough of thumbs!" Sforza roared. "Tell me what happened!"

"We followed the departing Balderdash fleet in order to ascertain where they were going, on the off-chance that they might come back again. They took a spiral route, north northwest toward the constellation of the Lattice, then east past the Grade Latrine, and then south again past the constellation of the Almond. After that...."

"I don't want to hear their whole bloody travel route!" Sforza said. "Where did they go, finally? Back to their own stupid little world, I suppose."

"No such thing, Sir," Kukri said quietly. "You know the black hole in Perseus Major?"

"Of course. Everyone knows that one."

"They went directly to that."

"Did they enter the black hole?"

"Yes, Sir. They disappeared below the event-horizon. And you know what that means."

"Of course I know," Sforza said. "The black hole leads to the Dark Universe."

"And that," Kukri said, "is their home."

"You can't be sure about that!" Sforza snapped.

"I can, Sire. Look at this." Kukri held out a handkerchief. There were several lumpy objects wrapped in it.

"What is it?" Sforza asked.

CHAPTER TWENTY-SIX

It was then that Alfonso brushed past the guards and stepped forward.

"And who are you?" Sforza demanded.

"My name is Alfonso," Alfonso said. "I am a minerals explorer for a large commercial company, and zygote-brother to Salvatore. But I am also a secret financial agent of the Central Government. We were on the trail of these." He took the handkerchief from Kukri and unfolded it. Inside were half a dozen gold coins.

"Well, they're just coins," said Sforza. "Gold, it looks like. What's the matter with that?"

"It is not real gold," Alfonso said.

"So it's fake gold?"

"Not that, either. This is anti-matter gold. It is gold identical to what we have in our universe, but with its particle charges reversed. It is also known as Contraterrene gold."

"Contraterrene matter," Sforza mused. "It is explosive when it comes into contact with normal matter, is it not?"

Alfonso nodded. "Gram for gram, CT matter is the most explosive substance in the universe."

"And you are saying that the Balderdash introduced

these coins into our universe?"

"That is correct, sir. We found these coins on Melchior. They had been brought in by the Balderdash to pay the expenses of their egg-substitution operation. They have no access to our universe's normal gold, because it's all in the hands of other people, but in their own antimatter universe, they can get unlimited quantities of it."

"'Why didn't this stuff blow up as soon as it got there?" Sforza asked.

"Feel the surface," Alfonso said, "Each coin is coated in Neutral Wax, a substance found only in the interface between their universe and ours. Using this wax, the gold will remain inert long enough for the Balderdash to spend it. But after a few months; the wax wears off and the coin explodes."

"But why were they doing all this?"

"It was their intention to implant their own race into our universe with a view to taking it over. They've already trashed their own universe and now want to fool around with ours. Melchior was the opening campaign, the thin edge of the wedge."

"And you knew all this?" Sforza asked.

Alfonso smiled. "We in Central Government have known it for a long time. They are insatiable, you know, the evil Balderdash beings of the dark universe."

"Their behavior," Toma said, "is like that of certain birds long known to the folklore of Earth. The cuckoo, who puts her eggs into other birds' nests, and the shrike, who impales birds on her long pointed beak.

The Balderdash combine the worst features of those two."

"It would have been a mess," Count Sforza said slowly.

"And you would have been responsible," Toma pointed out.

Soon thereafter, Count Sforza delivered his revised judgment. He had to admit that Sal had done well.

"You disobeyed my orders," he said, "but your instincts were good. It has all turned out very well. Princess Hatari, whose presence is expected momently, will be restored to the throne of Melchior. We'll sort out the technicalities later. And there'll be a raise in pay for you, Sal, and I'll promote you to bubaldar first-class."

The princess entered now, in a sweeping ballroom gown that accentuated her lush figure. Smiling sweetly, she said, "I, too, have a proposal to make to you, Sal. Perhaps you should hear me out before accepting the Count's offer."

"I'm listening," Sal said.

"I hereby propose a marriage between us," the princess said, blushing.

"I had not expected this," Sal said.

"I know it's a little sudden. But it makes sense. There's a way about you, Sal, that appeals to me. Frankly, I'm crazy about you. You will make a fine regent for the throne of Melchior."

"Princess," said Sal, "I must admit that I am not insensitive to your charms. But you forget the disparity in age between us."

"That is easy to take care of. You could take an Age Enhancement Package, or I could take an Age Slow-down Package. Either way, we could get together at appropriate ages."

"Hmm, interesting," Sal said.

Sforza said, "Now Sal, consider: Do you really want to leave the Sforza Condottieri? We could talk about a bonus, and a further jump in rank. When you wanted to marry, I could find a princess for you—one with a better planet to her dowry than Melchior."

"So he says," Hatari said. "But can you trust him? He was ready to exile you to Trabajo before even hearing your side!"

"And what about you?" Sforza said. "You wanted to use Sal to further your own ends!"

"Just a minute," Sal said. Turning to the princess, he said, "Hatari, you are a fine woman and you have made me a generous offer. But I think I'm not quite ready yet even to consider it. Give me some time. If the offer remains open, we can discuss it again in a year."

"I knew you'd see it my way," Sforza said.

"Not quite," Sal said. "Yes, I do want to continue as a fighting man of the Condottieri. It is the only trade I know. But first, I think I need some time off. I want to relax and be childish. Count, what I would really like is a year away from my duties. I'd like to spend that year on the Play Planet, for now that you have mentioned it, it intrigues me greatly. And I'd like you to pay for it."

"The Play Planet? But that's for kids!"

"I know, Sir. And I am something more than a kid, but something less, too. Give me a year to play, and then let me make my decision."

"And I," said Toma, "will accompany you to the Play Planet or wherever you go. We spider robots are faithful creatures."

"Well then," said the Count, "so be it. I will pay all your expenses, Sal. It is the least I can do for one who has saved our universe from the vile machinations of the Balderdash."

And so it was.

Sal left soon thereafter for the Play Planet, accompanied by the faithful Toma. What his decision would be at the end of a year, he did not know. That would come later. For now, there were new and wonderful games ahead of him, and that was sufficient for the present.

ABOUT THE AUTHOR

Robert Sheckley published some 60 books, mostly in the science fiction, fantasy, and mystery thriller genres. Several hundred of his stories appeared in the SF magazines, as well as in *Playboy, Omni, Ellery Queen, Alfred Hitchcock, Bluebook, Colliers*, and others. He wrote 60 stories for the radio series, *Behind the Green Door*, which were performed by actor Basil Rathbone for Monitor Radio. His first novel, *Immortality, Inc.* was produced as the movie *Freejack*, starring Mick Jagger and Anthony Hopkins. He also wrote the story, "7ᵗʰ Victim," which was the basis for the movie, *Tenth Victim*. His short story, "The Prize of Peril," was the basis for the French film, *La Prix du Danger*. A former *Omni* editor, Sheckley won the Jupiter Award in 1973, the Daniel F. Gallun Award for his contributions to the field of science fiction in 1991, and the Strannik Award in 1998. He was also named an Author Emeritus by the Science Fiction Writers of America. "The key words with Sheckley," says Spider Robinson, "are clever, deadly cool...I don't know anyone else in SF who has written quite so many really classic stories."

www.ingramcontent.com/pod-product-compliance
Lightning Source LLC
Chambersburg PA
CBHW020612260626
47157CB00003B/972

HUMAN'S BURDEN

Poor Jack Wong is a clueless cadet at the Unified Space Academy when his pod is stranded on a planet of disgusting aliens. All he wants to do, apart from escape, is fulfill his proud duty to advance Earth Culture's great Primary Heuristic: *Wherever possible, find the weak spot in an alien civilization and interfere as much as possible for the benefit of humanity.* It's the Human's Burden! But everything comes unstuck, made worse by his irritating Machiavellian AI. And that's just the start of Jack's troubles in space and time....

Borgo Press Books by DAMIEN BRODERICK

Chained to the Alien: The Best of ASFR: Australian SF Review (Second Series) [Editor]

Climbing Mount Implausible: The Evolution of a Science Fiction Writer

Embarrass the Dog: The Way We Were, the Things We Thought

Ferocious Minds: Polymathy and the New Enlightenment

Human's Burden (with Rory Barnes)

I'm Dying Here (with Rory Barnes)

Skiffy and Mimesis: More Best of ASFR: Australian SF Review (Second Series) [Editor]

Unleashing the Strange: Twenty-First Century Science Fiction Literature

Warriors of the Tao [Editor with Van Ikin]

x, y, z, t: Dimensions of Science Fiction

Borgo Press Books by RORY BARNES

The Dragon Raft: A Young Adult Novel

Human's Burden (with Damien Broderick)

I'm Dying Here (with Damien Broderick)

HUMAN'S BURDEN

A SCIENCE FICTION NOVEL

DAMIEN BRODERICK &

RORY BARNES

THE BORGO PRESS
MMX

HUMAN'S BURDEN

Copyright © 2010 by Damien Broderick and
Rory Barnes

FIRST EDITION

Published by Wildside Press LLC

www.wildsidebooks.com

DEDICATION

To Brigadier General Livick
For advice both valuable
and invaluable

And to the memory of
Robert Sheckley
and Douglas Adams

CONTENTS

INTRODUCTION

Here is my hypothesis as to how Human's Burden came to be written. Keith Laumer and Gene Roddenberry were sitting around one day, stoned out of their gourds on *ayahuasca*. They decided to stitch the head of interstellar diplomat James Retief onto the body of Captain James T. Kirk—or vice versa. The hybrid, supremely handsome and conceited monster sat in cryonic suspension for forty years until Broderick and Barnes found and activated him with a hypodermic containing a mixture of Robert Sheckley's and Ron Goulart's stem cells, and then the two Aussie authors simply chronicled the revenant's adventures.

Or, alternatively, applying Occam's Razor, Broderick and Barnes are just stone-cold comic science-fictional geniuses. Take your pick.

—Paul Di Filippo,
author of *Roadside Bodhisattva*

CHAPTER ONE
ALIENS

The aliens stank, even from all the way across the clearing. And they were making a really terrible noise.

They sang out at the top of their voices with shrieking gusto, and the vented gases that puffed from the slots in their snouts smelled vile. Jack Wong watched the aliens cavort about, working themselves into a hot frenzy. The sweat glands under their tails sent a fetid stench billowing toward him.

Whatever they were cooking over the red and yellow fire was rotten, and green maggots crawled hastily out of it before crisping and falling into the flames, but the aliens didn't care. Two of them stood in the heat turning the decayed carcass on a spit, and drool fell from their slimy snouts to spit and hiss in the fire.

"I'm going to puke," Jack said, trying to breathe through his mouth. He had his fingers clamped over his nose. It didn't help much; he could still smell the foul thing they were roasting in the roaring fire. Whatever it had been when it was alive, it had been dead far too long. He'd seen it hanging from a hook in the hot sunlight all this last week, and he had a revolted

feeling they were going to make him eat some of it, once it was cooked.

An offering to their new god.

"If you are going to be sick, Jack," his on-board AI said sternly, "try not to get any inside your suit."

Jack shuddered. Even with his helmet open, it would be messy. No easy way to clean up vomit. He gulped hard and tried not to think about how nauseated he felt.

"Any signal from the rescue detail yet?" he asked the Machiavellian intelligence. He could hear the whine in his own voice, and it made him angry. He was an interstellar cadet, after all, not a sniveling adolescent. He'd turned nineteen years old a month ago, and he was a fully trained pod pilot, holding the Unified Academy rank of Cadet Master Chief Petty Officer. It was hardly his fault the Arcturus wormhole had belched at the wrong moment and hurled his pod halfway across the galaxy, or wherever the hell he was now, and dropped him here on some planet nobody had ever—

"Sir, you will certainly be the first to know if I detect a response to our emergency signal." The system was not being sarcastic; Jack was convinced the AI had zero sense of humor. Not that his own was in full running order right now. Stuck here on a disgusting alien planet with a barely breathable atmosphere and an AI that acted like a prissy nanny, the sort he and his sister Gillian had shared when they were kids in the General Francisco Paulino Hermenegildo Teódulo Franco y Bahamonde Salgado Pardo de Andrade Memorial Kindergarten. That seemed a very long time

ago. Now Gillian was an expert alien anthropologist.

Jack's neck was itching horribly. His gloved fingers were too thick to fit inside the opening of his helmet, but he couldn't take the gloves off without shucking his entire suit. He prodded at the rash under the edge of his helmet with a dry purple stick that had fallen from a tree resembling a giant anteater. The living branches of the tree, or maybe it was a bush, had in fact been swaying back and forth, scooping up and eating slow creatures that might have been rather large ants.

As he delved under the helmet, the purple stick hit a particularly sensitive scab and its end snapped off, tumbled down into the back of his suit and jammed itself there, jabbing his prickling skin. Oh, great. He'd started with an itch he couldn't scratch, and now as a bonus he had a sharp pain halfway down his spine from the broken stick. Jack said a word prohibited on 53 worlds, and threw the rest of the twig back on the messy floor of his cell. Or his hut, or his shrine, or whatever the superstitious aliens thought it was.

"Your cortisol stress levels are rising again, Jack. Perhaps you should lie down for a while and do some math homework. Here, I will run off some ballistic curves for you to study."

A series of bright lines sprang into place in Jack's left eye, projected from the AI perched on the back on his suit. A list of delta-vee equations ran down beside the crisscrossing lines. He knew what they were, he wasn't a complete fool, after all. Delta-vee, that was... that was— That was change of velocity, of course it

was, a very important thing to have mastered when you were trying to pilot a lost pod that had tumbled with hardly any anti-gravitino fuel toward an unknown planet in the middle of nowhere. He blinked angrily, shutting off the education display.

"For the love of sanity, Mac! They're about to roast me alive, and you expect me to think about class?"

"If you had paid more attention to your lessons, sir," the AI said patiently, "we might not be in this difficult situation now."

"I knew it!" The cadet lurched back to his feet, furious and indignant. "You're blaming me for getting the wormhole insertion wrong! You did the calculations!"

"You, however, are the human space cadet, sir." Jack could never win an argument with the machine. It had, after all, a mind like a computer. "The responsibility is ultimately yours, sir," the Mac was saying. "I am no more than your assistant and lowly tutor."

"Ha!" And goddam nanny. And, on this world, translator. The Mac had analyzed the aliens' local dialect within minutes of their crash landing, and could bleat and bark back at them with all the ease of a native speaker. Of course the machine got some of the words wrong, and left a few more out altogether. It is hard for a human to understand an alien, and just as hard for an alien to see what a human is trying to say, even with an effective translating AI as your go-between.

Jack knew this much: The stenchy aliens thought he was a god. He just hoped that he wasn't the sort

of god that worshippers put to death. If only he had advice from Dr. Fisherking. Or his best friend in the Academy, fellow cMaster Chief Rufus Rupert Trevor Dogge. Or Cadet Ensign Hortense Jones. *She'd* know what to do, with her being so smart and all. Even given the mess he was in, that whole thing with Jones' rank still stuck in his craw.

He swallowed with a gulp. In the whole universe, Jack Wong was probably the hungriest god in captivity. And the most frightened.

∞

Ten days earlier, he'd managed to drag his pod onto circular orbit around this torrid jungle planet that baked just a little too close to its hot bluish sun. Well, actually it was the artificial intelligence system who'd done the most boring parts of piloting their way onto orbit, but that's what it was for, after all. Jack spent a full day and a half spinning around the planet, finding out as much as he could at long range about the world's geography, ecology and especially its dominant life form. Its native inhabitants were aliens, of course, because no human had ever come this way before. Chances were, given how horribly lost he and the pod were, none ever would again. A couple of times he'd found himself weeping, and once he just broke down in a fit of shivering terror. The AI pulled him out of it each time, with its eerie calm tones.

The pod's automatics broke out a series of excellent instruments from the hull, and pointed them at

the whirling hot planet, sucking in data that the system patiently stored and sorted into files that only a machine could care about. His polariton telescope brought him vivid images of the small shifting settlements where the native aliens lived. There were many different kinds of habitat, of course, because a world is a large place. Still, he detected no radio messages, no hints of power generation or even large-scale water irrigation and dams, or roads, or wheeled carriages. The swarming vegetation of the planetary jungle seemed to have closed out some of those options. Jack realized—recalling his history lessons in the Academy—that unless some external influence came into the picture, this world's intelligent inhabitants would need to wait for a change of climate before they built their Romes, their Babylons, their Jerichos. An ice age or two, that's what they needed. Jack had squinted at the glaring bluish star that was their sun. Not much chance of that.

Under normal circumstances, Jack Wong would have been studying to act as just that external influence. No doubt about it, from the time he'd graduated from Paul Joseph Goebbels High School at the age of seventeen, he'd been getting ready to share in the greatest and grandest adventure humankind had ever seen. He would follow Earth Culture's great Primary Heuristic: *Wherever possible, find the weak spot in an alien civilization and interfere as much as possible for the benefit of humanity.* Deliberate imperial intervention was the name of the game. Humans, luckily, had found the methods of science and correct psychology

centuries ago, and it was their duty—*his* duty, in this case—to carry this wonderful knowledge across the galaxy to all the beings who lacked it, and bring them into the imperium, kicking and screaming if need be. Wiping them out entirely was frowned on these days.

Imperial Earth Culture had been spreading through the galaxy for more than two centuries, following prospector Amanda Bufon's discovery of the first known wormhole in the asteroid belt, on the far side of Mars and nearly to Jupiter. That's where the Academy was located nowadays, in a grand set of habitat bubbles just a thousand kilometers from Wormhole One. Jack had spent happy teenage years there, getting his spacelegs, learning how Earth Culture was welding the universe into a league of peaceful species. So far they had never found a civilization quite as advanced as Earth's, though a few had space travel and powerful weapons. Artful negotiation for trading rights had done the trick in nearly every case—there hadn't been need for a genocidal war, Jack's instructors told him proudly, for more than a hundred years.

Whirling lost and confused above the unknown planet in his pod, Jack Wong had kept his head. With the AI system's help, he readied a swarm of spy probes disguised to resemble a local insect. Ugly things, he thought with a shudder, but then suppressed his reaction. He was the visitor here, even if he hadn't planned to be. It was up to him to fit in, for the moment. However horrible the local life forms seemed, Earth Culture lore had taught him, he was to take a deep breath and step

forth boldly to greet them as a leader and adviser. This was his proud duty as a human being from Earth. By comparison with some of these backward aliens he was almost a god, but he shouldn't let it go to his head. The Primary Heuristic was the guiding principle of the empire.

Jack Wong fired the myriad tiny probes into the atmosphere. They dispersed, humming to themselves. Quite soon they sent back a great supply of local sights and sounds to the pod's AI system, and it was the work of only an hour or two for the machine to select a suitable continent, listen to the weird screeches and bubblings the aliens used as a language, and crack the basics of its vocabulary and grammar. By the time Jack Wong had got up enough nerve to go down to the surface, his translating module was ready for service, awaiting only a fine tuning for the local dialect. Just as well, he'd told himself with a wry grin. He certainly couldn't have made any sense of the jibber-jabber by himself.

He'd landed his pod in the early morning, so most of the aliens were up and about, getting ready for a day's hunting and gathering. The pod came down in a clearing off to one side of the village, blasting brush and purple roots and rocks with the hot flame of the landing venturis. Luckily the jungle vegetation was wet with the clinging humidity of the whole planet, except for the cooler poles of course, so no major fires were started. Several sad cases were on record of Earth Culture spacecraft incinerating the first village they

tried to contact, so now foam fire extinguishers were standard fitting on all landers.

Jack Wong had climbed free of his landing web and activated the outside cameras and microphones. In his viewing screen, aliens were swarming toward the pod, shouting to each other and gesticulating wildly. At a cautious distance, they ground to a halt, consulting with each other in a shrieking babble. The noise set Jack's teeth on edge. One or two held primitive weapons they'd been carrying when the pod came crashing down, but none of them appeared to be menacing the craft.

Oh well. He might be lost thousands of light years from home, but this was the job he was in training to do. Heart swelling with a mixture of pride and sheer terror, he said aloud, "I'll have the suit now, thanks."

"You feel quite ready to go outside?" the AI system asked him. "There's no rush, you know."

Jack's stomach jumped. "You haven't had a signal from—?"

Regretfully, the AI told him, "No. I am still unable to establish contact with the empire. I will keep trying. Meanwhile, you should feel under no obligation to leave the safety of this pod. You could continue your ballistic lessons from the comfort of your—"

"No, no," Jack said hastily. "Really, it's my duty to make First Contact with these people. I'll have the suit, thanks."

It took several minutes of bending and twisting to get into the rigid frame of the protective garment. His right foot started to itch just between the big toe and its

neighbor the moment he closed the final seal. Jack took a deep breath, opened the airlock, stepped outside onto the scorched ground.

A muffled muttering spread among the aliens, then screams and shrieks, and they fell down on their faces before him.

"Oh my god!" Appalled, Jack Wong took a step back, pressed against the warm hull. His very presence had killed them all! The aliens lay stretched out in front of him like swatted flies. No, they weren't dead yet, a twitch or two and the blink of a beady eye proved they were still alive. He sagged in relief, then stiffened again in fresh panic. What had he done to cause this? Everything he'd learned in months of Contact training deserted him. The aliens stayed where they were, heads down and tails up, and they moaned. A silly giggle caught in Jack's throat, but he sternly forced it down. This was no time for laughter. He had no idea what to do. Not the faintest clue.

"I'm coming back in," he told the pod.

"Not advisable," said the Mac, his suit's on-board AI and translator. Its voice was slightly deeper than the pod's AI system, to which it was connected. "You have been neglecting your studies, sir. If you had paid closer attention during the lesson on *Alien species, Obeisance of,* you would know exactly what to do."

Jack's consternation grew. "Obey what?" he squeaked.

"Obeisance," the Mac repeated. "Oh-bay-zance," it added more slowly, emphasizing each part of the unfa-

miliar word. "It means a submissive gesture of respect. To be brutally frank, they are worshipping you."

"Me?" Jack Wong's voice squealed even higher. Luckily the aliens couldn't hear his foolish tones, since his suit's helmet was soundproof. Everything he heard came to his ears through the Mac's microphones, and when he decided it was time to talk to the fallen aliens his voice would be translated into...into *alien*...by the on-board AI. "Why would they worship *me*? I'm just a human from Earth!"

"On occasion," the Mac informed him, "primitive alien peoples will mistake Earth Culture personnel for religious figures from their own mythologies."

"What, they think I'm a sky god?"

"Or a demon, ghoul, vampire, harpy, or other monster. They must be disabused of this notion as rapidly as possible. Only after personnel have established themselves as equally mortal can the process of cultural orientation begin."

"So you're telling me," Jack said slowly, stepping cautiously away from the hull toward the stirring aliens, "you're saying that— That they probably do think I'm a god, but I should tell them I'm not, right?"

"Exactly." Was there just a trace of impatient scorn in the machine's voice? "Then we can start carrying out the Primary Heuristic and begin helping these aliens on their rise to near-equality with humankind."

All the aliens were on their feet by now, milling about. One of them raised a spear in what looked like a menacing gesture.

"Well, all right." Jack raised his suited head bravely and stepped forward. "Tell them my name is Jack Wong and that I'm very happy to be here on their beautiful planet."

The sound system in his helmet rang across the clearing in the Mac's voice, speaking some kind of alien gibberish. The eyes bugged in their buggy heads, and they stared for a brief moment at Jack with open snouts.

This time, it wasn't so unnerving when they cast themselves on the ground again.

Jack's scalp was itching, and he wondered if he should take off his helmet and have a good scratch. It seemed the wrong moment for that. "Er, now, look here, fellows," he said, and the Mac barked and squawked out an instant translation of his words in alien. "Don't keep doing that, please. It can't be healthy, slithering around like that in the wet grass."

The aliens bounded back a few more meters, bowing and scraping and muttering incoherently. So far the Mac had not provided Jack with a translation of anything they were saying. "I am sorry," it told him, "we shall have to wait until they calm down, I cannot make any sense of that hubbub."

Jack Wong gazed unhappily at the writhing bodies before him, and wished with all his might that he were back in the Academy, or better still home on Earth. He felt as if he'd burst out bawling any second. Instead, he squared his shoulders and prepared to utter the Traditional Greeting.

"Take me to your leader," he said, and the Mac coughed out the alien words. "I wish to speak to someone in authority. One of your, uh, Wise Men, Women or Things." Nervously, he rubbed his gloved hands together.

The aliens conferred. Finally a shrunken oldster wobbled hesitantly toward Jack. Its features were more pitted than the rest, its drool greener, gelatinous. When it spoke, its voice was cracked and wheezy.

The Mac said, "That probably meant something like: 'O King, live forever!' But more like a god than a king, if you see what I mean."

"Oh shit," Jack moaned, wishing he could rub his nose.

∞

Their village was no more impressive from the ground than it had been through the sensors from orbit. Less than a hundred small grass huts, cunningly built to keep the heavy rain out but hardly beautiful. Still, he told himself, that was only to be expected of a species that had to keep on the move in search of game. Probably they needed to keep cutting back the encroaching jungle, make new clearings that would be swallowed a few months later when they shifted to fresh territory.

Grawnkar, the old alien, apparently their leader, hobbled along half a step behind Jack, and rest trailed after. As they entered the village, other large adult aliens (the mothers? but he didn't even know how

many sexes the aliens had, or if they had any at all) and small squealing alien children emerged from huts and gardens to gape in open-mouthed amazement. In the middle of the scattered huts two structures rose above the rest. Jack was herded toward one, perhaps the chieftain's home or headquarters. The other was a tall palisade, sturdier than the rest, its round wall made of solid timber stakes with nasty thorns jutting out, its entrance flanked by carved poles showing a certain artistic skill. A temple of some sort?

Jack eyed it with distaste. The very thought of these people's gods reminded him of how hard it would be to convince them he was not unlike them in his mortality and limitations, despite the difference in their appearance. Human or alien, he'd been taught by Earth Culture instructors, it was all one, really, once they were cleaned up and properly indoctrinated. Yes, he might seem to the poor benighted creatures to have godlike powers. He'd come down out of the sky, after all. But when all was said and done, he was exactly as mortal as they, and he needed to get this idea across to them as quickly as possible. Jack Wong squared his shoulders deliberately, and marched into Grawnkar's hut.

∞

"You don't understand," he told the puzzled aliens for the tenth time. "I'm just like you. Cut me, do I not bleed? Not," he added hurriedly, "that I want you to cut me. Heck forbid."

His voice was hoarse, and he was getting hungry. The suit had a store of rations, but they weren't very tasty. In fact, they tasted like sawdust. You weren't meant to enjoy lazing around on strange planets in a comfortable survival suit; the idea was to get in, get the job of Contact done, and get out again, all as expeditiously as possible. It was a big galaxy out there, and Contact was a never-ending job. Unfortunately, the aliens seemed to have taken a fancy to Jack. They seemed to regard him as something of a prize. A sort of trophy. Their own little tin god. How embarrassing.

"The sky god mocks us," said old Grawnkar. "You look nothing like a mortal."

"But—but—" It was no good. Jack threw up his hands in despair. He'd tried again and again to explain through his translator that small difference in color and size—well, even really big differences, in this case— didn't amount to the difference between a mortal and god. This just got such a puzzled reception that Jack lapsed into angry silence and chewed his lip for a quarter of an hour.

"I am going to have to turn the cooling system off," the Mac murmured in his ear. "We are running low on power."

"You can't do that!" Jack cried in alarm. "I'll roast! I'll boil in my own juices."

"You can always take your helmet off."

"Yeah, right, and catch some horrible disease."

"The chances are very low that an alien disease or fungus could thrive on a human body," the translator

told him smugly, "or in one."

∞

When night finally fell, a haze of stars in no known constellations twinkling above the clearing, it was hardly any cooler. The cooking fire the alien monsters built made it worse. Insect things he'd emulated for his spy probes swarmed out of the humming forest and annoyed him by biting his unprotected neck and face. The fallen stick fragment jabbed his spine in a different place every time he moved. He glanced at his glove's fingerwatch, wondering how soon he'd be able to make his apologies and slip away for a comfortable night's rest in the air-conditioned pod. Grawnkar sidled up in the dark

"O Jack Wong," the translated voice said respectfully, "the feast begins. If you would grace it by your illustrious presence, we would be blessed beyond repayment."

What could he do? Jack shrugged, stuck his helmet under his arm and made his way to the place of honor. The closer he got to the fire, the worse it stank. He gagged, tried hard not to throw up. That could cause a diplomatic incident. It certainly would not look good on his academic record, or his official report for that matter.

If he ever got home. If the Earth Culture rescue team ever tracked him through the wormhole and found him here before he grew old and frail and white haired, and died of old age. A tear of self-pity crept from his eye,

and an insect buzzed down with sharp feet to sip at it.

Everyone was guzzling with gusto, chatting away in their awful voices, except for two ceremonial guards behind him. His stomach growled hungrily. Oh, why not? If the bugs couldn't hurt him, maybe the food wouldn't either? It smelled disgusting, but you could get used to anything. And he might be here for a long time. He eyed a particularly choice piece of blue vegetation, or maybe it was meat or fish, from the huge pile before him and reached out one gloved hand.

A huge wooden club whistled down from behind his right ear and thudded into the dirt not a centimeter from his fingers.

Stunned with fright, Jack whipped back his hand and sat stock-still for a long moment. All the chatter had stopped. Interested reptilian eyes peered at the sky god who had very nearly lost his fingers. Old Grawnkar leaned over, his breath like something from a garbage can, and said reprovingly, "It is not fitting for the sky god to be associated with the fruits of the offering, nor even his bearer. Time enough later, for the god, when the first-fruits are burned and ascend as fumes to the sky."

∞

The palisade, when they lit smoky torches and took Jack inside, was not uncomfortable. The floor was covered with dried grass and in one corner he found a reasonably soft cot of rushes. But the walls were thick and solid, and the guard stood at the opening. And

there was no food or drink.

Jack felt tears come to his eyes again, and he brushed them aside. With his tongue, he triggered the lever than brought a trickle of sawdust-flavored nutrient into his mouth, and a squirt of warm water. Luckily, the suit was able to retrieve his bodily wastes and recycle them into sawdust-flavored nutrient and warm water.

They kept him there for eight days.

∞

The racket outside rose in a pitch of excitement. Red and yellow flames burst up from the fire. Big flat alien feet with scaly toenails pounded on the packed dirt of the camp's central square.

Nervously, Jack edged closer to the sturdy wooden gate of the shrine he was imprisoned inside. Through a chink between crudely carved planks, he saw twenty or thirty of the appalling creatures stamping and waving and bowing and hollering as the sparks flew up into the darkening sky. Every now and then, the old one with the dark green scaly spots on its underbelly turned toward his prison/shrine and bleated in a high, thin yodel. The Mac had stopped automatically translating when Jack found it all too depressing. The other aliens turned and bobbed, waving horrible weapons with sharp ends. Jack felt sick again.

"I have acquired a signal," the Mac told him.

The cadet sagged with relief.

"Unfortunately, the Primary Heuristic forbids the rescue craft from landing in plain view of the local

aliens. You will have to make your way by foot four kilometers south-east of the clearing where we crashed. Lt. Commandant Lawson and his crew will collect us and dispose of the damaged pod."

"Great," Jack said. "Wonderful plan. And how am I supposed to get out of this place? The gate's locked, remember? No windows." He made his way in the gloom to a plank at the base of the wall that he had been loosening for several days with his gloved hands. With a shove, he pushed it free. The space it left would be barely enough for him to crawl through without his suit.

He was chilled at the thought.

"If I take off the suit, I'll have no protection against their weapons," he said, shaking slightly.

"They will not necessarily kill you," the Mac said. "They believe you are a sky god, after all. That is why they are holding this sacred ceremony in your honor. By the way, I gather they wish you to join them shortly for the festivities, and those could continue for many hours and entail certain dangers to a human. Now would be the time to depart."

"But I'd have to leave you behind," Jack said with a terrified sob. He was stripping open the heavy suit, his exposed skin burning slightly as the planet's unearthly mix of gases stung him. The itch on his neck worsened, and started to spread down his chest, where it blended with a river of cold sweat. The Machiavellian intelligence sat seamlessly welded into the back of his helmet, a bright box of tricks with lenses, external

speaker and retractable antennae. There was no way Jack could cut or pull the AI free.

"Just leave me," the AI said in a flat machine voice. "I will terminate my program the moment you are off the surface."

Jack shrugged, shoved the mound of his empty suit aside. It was a little strange, hearing the Mac speak from down there on the floor, rather than in his ear. That must be how the aliens heard the machine's voice as it translated their barks and whistles.

"Okay, Mac. Thank you for everything."

"My pleasure, sir, and my duty."

Grunting, the cadet wriggled through the narrow gap. He paused for a moment to watch the capering aliens. Abruptly, the noises stopped. In the silence, one of the five-legged creatures turned and gestured at the shrine. Jack's heart accelerated in terror. They had seen him outside the hut! They might revere him as a fallen sky god, but they wanted to hang on to their new divinity. Certainly they would not allow him to escape back into the heavens! The Mac had made that very clear.

With a whoop, the whole tribe cantered around the roaring fire and pressed toward the barred gate of the shrine. Jack screamed in fright, bolted upright in plain sight of them, and ran in his underwear into the jungle.

Nobody followed him.

At the dark edge of the alien forest, the cadet paused long enough to look warily back at the shrine. The aliens had thrown open the gate, and the old one was

trotting back and forth in front of the fire in triumph, holding something shapeless and heavy over its head. It looked like a human corpse, squashed horribly by a trampling elephant.

"Oh god," Jack muttered, "that could have been me."

Two of the aliens fetched out a framework of sticks and arranged the empty space suit over it, so that it stood up in front of the ritual flames like a sagging scarecrow. The Mac's box gleamed in the firelight, and its lenses shone. The uplink antenna slowly extruded like a snail's tentacle. The aliens paused, ceased their commotion, fell silent. A new voice spoke, a stern mix of barks and whistles. The aliens fell down on their many knees and placed their bulbous heads in the dust.

Jack gasped, stared, and then started to laugh.

He couldn't help himself. He giggled, and sniggered, and finally roared out loud.

None of this noise attracted the distant attention of the aliens. They were perfectly happy, worshipping their god, the sky creature that had fallen into their world and spoke to them in their own tongue.

Jack turned, still smiling, and slunk into the undergrowth. He had four kilometers to cover to the waiting rescue ship. As he moved away, the powerful voice called out to him from the clearing, in his own human language.

"Goodbye, young Jack," the Mac called. "Good luck, human. You made a very satisfactory horse."

Jack grinned, shaking his head. The aliens had never been interested in him at all. They had worshipped his

machine, his AI, his micronic nanny. And now they would do so forever, without the inconvenience of dealing with their god's strangely shaped two legged, two armed steed.

A hour later, the rescue pod flashed a light at him, and Jack wondered how he would explain all this to Commandant Whimsel back at the Academy. Probably best to say as little as possible. Human colonists would get an almighty surprise, though, when they finally returned to this world in a few centuries' time....

CHAPTER TWO
AN OTHER WORLD ZOO

Jack's Academy Company (Co. 505) had been rotated back to their home world for R&R, quartered in a dull corner of Spaceport Earth. They were paid a vacation allowance of 1,000 yuans and warned not to blow it all the first night on booze, strippers or fancy men, unlikely investments and other foolishness. Jack found this advice so intimidating that he mostly stayed home and slept for fourteen hours a day in his quarters, waking every night from frightful nightmares of aliens dancing by a fire and a Machiavellian AI on his back.

The rest of the time, when he wasn't cadging extra rations from the loud, happy Brazilian cook in the officer's mess, he spent playing Warcraft Worlds or reading his email. To his frustration he did not get much email, even from Gillian, his more intellectual sister, and most of what did show up was spam. He was bored, so bored that eventually he gave way and started reading the spam. Nobody in their right mind would fall for offers of five trillion yuans from the Nigerian moonunit, but there were more subtle temptations. Jack Wong had always been a sucker for a garage sale, so when he

opened a plain email addressed to him personally, an email that said only *Monster Garage Sale—Hangar 51,* he was there like a nail to a magnet.

Hangar 51 was the fabled treasure store where crashed flying saucers, recovered artifacts from Atlantis and other lost civilizations, alien mechanisms and the Ark of the Covenant were alleged to be stored. Jack floogled it and the map directed him to 27 Wilson Street. He hitched a lift most of the way and walked the last couple of blocks, his heart slowly sinking.

He stopped at last. He stared about. The whole street was dilapidated, absurdly so for a military base. No power weapons mounted behind razor wire, no crack guard units marching back and forth protecting incredible secrets. Number 27 was unlike any hangar he'd ever seen. It was an old, falling down house behind a high, overgrown hedge. In the front yard he saw a leaning *For Sale* sign. Grass grew in the gutters. Frankly, Jack wasn't surprised that the owners were moving out. He'd have moved out too. An old military man in a silver lycra jumpsuit full of holes sat in a rocking chair on the veranda, looking almost as old and broken down as the house.

Jack took a second look, then stared in disbelief. This was no bum crashing in a deserted barracks. He recognized one of the most famous men in all space: Rear Admiral Ricardo Fortesque Martinique (ret.). He snapped to attention, and held a smart salute.

"Admiral Martinique, *sir!*"

The admiral peered down, spat out a wad of chaw,

threw a half salute in answer, and cackled. "At ease, Cadet Ensign Wong. Welcome, welcome, my young friend. Come right on in, don't loiter. There are more treasures here than can be found in all the spaceship wrecks under all the stars."

"You know who I am?" Jack blurted, still afraid to move. "Sir?"

"Obviously, or how could I have sent you that invitation to the Monster Garage Sale? Oh, and also you were in the news last year after that imbroglio with the Grawnks."

"Yes, sir," Jack said, with an involuntary shudder, not at all sure he liked the way this was headed. Wherever that was. He walked up the path, and burrs from the overgrown weeds caught at his ankles. He went up the paint-peeling steps, which creaked.

If it hadn't been for all the stuff laid out on trestle tables, the disguised Hangar 51 would have given him the creeps. Not to mention the ancient officer himself and his disturbing talk of starship wrecks and the way he knew Jack's name and email address. But Jack shook off his mood of apprehension. Now he was here, he was too interested in grabbing a bargain to worry about how freaky things were. There was some good stuff on the tables, that was true. He felt the unspent yuans in his billfold, yearning to be spent on something wild and unique.

There were old clocks for all the planets of the solar system, and some beyond. None of them worked, but Jack felt sure he could have a great time taking them

apart and rebuilding them. Another table held a collection of military hats and strange jewelry gleaming with precious stones from far-flung star systems, or maybe just colored glass. His hands ran lightly over little wood and brass boxes, shuffled peculiar packs of cards with odd markings. He'd be able to buy some stuff for himself and some to trade with Annie Tan. Her parents ran an elite restaurant and between them they made the best lunches in the galaxy. As a result Annie was a butter ball, endlessly trying to diet. And the other cadets of the Company tried to help her—by eating her lunch. In fact there was so much demand for Annie's lunch that she didn't just give it away, she traded it. Jack was going to be the lucky trader.

He purchased a little wood and brass box to trade with Annie, a broken down clock to dismantle, and a Martian ring with a Martian skull on it. The ring looked silver, but might have been an ancient synthetic whose formula was lost in the sands of Mars. He pushed the ring on his finger as the Admiral packed the rest neatly in a recyclable bag. Jack saluted smartly and awaited a return salute so he could leave.

"Wait a moment, cadet. Want to buy a raffle ticket?"

A *raffle* ticket? He hadn't heard of a raffle since he was a child. He dropped the salute, figuring the Admiral wasn't interested. "How much, Sir?" He still had twenty yuans left.

"Twenty yuans," said the Admiral, producing a book of tickets.

There was not much you could buy for twenty

yuans. Jack bought a raffle ticket, although he knew he wouldn't win. Even as a kid, Jack had never won raffles.

"I'll need your billet address, my young friend. In case you win."

∞

The following day, Jack traded the little box for all of Annie's lunch, and it was scrumptious. Lieutenant Zamblott, the commissioned officer in charge of Company 505, was absent on sick leave, having lost a leg during an incident that never made the news. Jack told the other cadets in his company about the Monster Garage sale and Rear Admiral Ricardo Fortesque Martinique (ret.), to the disbelieving derision of cadet Lieutenant Julia Durango and her claque. Julia and cLt. Hortense Jones outranked Jack Wong and Rufus Rupert Trevor Dogge by virtue of academic merit, even though, according to the male cadets, they couldn't fly as well. And they missed no opportunity to pull rank. Jack gritted his teeth and said nothing about the raffle ticket, mentioning it only to Annie Tan and his friend Rufus, who said, "So what's the prize?"

"Don't know," Jack said. "I never asked."

"Give us a look at the ticket."

Jack fished the ticket out of his pocket and they studied it, but there was no mention of what the prize was. The only thing written on the ticket was a number. The number was 001.

"So you got the first ticket," Annie said. "Maybe 001

is a lucky number."

"Maybe it isn't," Jack said. His unpleasant experiences with the aliens the year before had not encouraged a spirit of optimism.

∞

As Jack turned the corner into the street fronting the Company's quarters, a large truck with a crane on the back floated away from the curb. As it passed, the driver waved. Jack waved back. The sign on the truck's door said *We Cart Anything Co.*

Jack blinked when he reached the front gate, then stood and stared at the large dome someone had erected on the front lawn, half covering the rose bush. Lt. Zamblott would go apeshit, whereupon Jack would surely and unfairly suffer. Had the truck driver unloaded the thing?

He couldn't make sense of it. Neither Lt. Zamblott nor CLt. Jones had mentioned a new installation. Besides, they wouldn't have put it slap bang in the middle of the front lawn. Admittedly, that might be a typical example of military intelligence. Actually, it looked like a garage for a flivver. A personal flivver. CLts. Durango and Annie Tan were the only young people on base with family wealthy enough for a flivver. Jack shook his head. Lt. Zamblott was going to *shit,* and Jack knew he could count on standing a few mid-to-4 watches because of it.

"A very handsome structure," said a voice behind him.

Jack spun round, snapped to attention. "Admiral Martinique!"

"At ease, lad. You've got to stop doing that, it's wearing on an old man's nerves."

"Sir, what's that thing doing here?"

"It's not doing anything," the old man said. "It's just standing still."

"I can see that, sir," Jack said. "You're absolutely right. It's not moving. But why is it here?"

"It's here because you won it."

"*I* won it? I *won* it?"

"Ticket number 001 was the winning ticket," said the Admiral. "Congratulations, my young friend, you have won a Garage Monster."

"Sir, you mean a Monster Garage. I don't want a Monster Garage," Jack said. "Lt. Zamblott will go ape."

"It's yours," said the famous oldster. "You bought a raffle ticket at a Monster Garage sale, and consequently you've won a Garage Monster. Now, if you'll excuse me, I must be off."

He started to hobble away, putting a lot of weight on his walking stick.

"Hang on, sir," Jack said. "Please, not so fast."

"Alas," said Rear Admiral Ricardo Fortesque Martinique (ret.), coming to a halt, "it is many years since I could go fast."

"Look," Jack said, thinking quickly. "You say that's meant to be a Monster Garage, right? First prize in the raffle was a Monster Garage?"

"That is correct."

"Well," Jack said. "It is only an *ordinary* sized garage. You could only fit one flivver in there. It is not a Monster Garage. Please arrange to have it taken away."

"Size has nothing to do with it," said the Admiral.

"Sir, the size has everything to do with it," Jack said. "The prize was meant to be a Monster Garage and that garage is not monstrous."

"Tell me," the admiral said, "what would you expect to find in a boat shed?"

Jack was confused. "A boat?"

"Correct. And what would you expect to find in a hay barn?"

"Hay, I guess."

"Correct. And in a tool shed? A cow shed? A tram depot? A pig sty? A dog house?"

"Sir, tools, cows, trams, pigs, dogs," Jack said, increasingly annoyed.

"What," said the old gentleman, "would you expect to find in a Monster Garage?"

"You're shitting me," Jack said. "Sir."

"No, I'm not," said the Admiral, and turned once more and hobbled away.

∞

Jack walked slowly round the outside of the garage. It was sealed. He wasn't going to try to open it until he knew what was inside. Luckily he found a small, high window on the far side, directly above the Diana, Princess of Wales roses, their cream with pink blush horrible crushed. Jack went inside and got a chair to

stand on. He looked down through the garage window and almost fell off the chair.

The monster was...monstrous. It looked like a scaly Kodiak bear with a distinct resemblance to a goat, and there was a touch of the silverback gorilla about it. Its face, it seemed suddenly to Jack, looked a bit like Lt. Zamblott's. Surely this was not some frightful medical accident, or—No. When the monstrous alien caught sight of him, it let out a roar and jumped at the window, foaming at the mouth. Jack did fall off the chair then, and scrambled away. The monster alien hammered on the walls with its great scaled paws. Or maybe it was kicking with its feet. Or both. Jack Wong was in no mood to try to find out by taking another look. The garage vibrated with the sounds of the monster alien's roaring. People in and out of uniform started to gather in the street. Jack went inside hastily and shut the door.

∞

CLt. Jones said, "Cadets, the first thing we should do is have a word with Rear Admiral Ricardo Fortesque Martinique. You can't just raffle monster aliens. There must be laws against it."

Jones and Jack ordered immediate delivery of a flivver from the motor pool and within minutes jumped to 27 Wilson Street. It was getting dark, but this time a guard stood in the decaying garden watering dying flowers with a hose. The enlisted man was about Jack's age and neatly dressed in working uniform. He saluted, said, "Good evening, ma'am," and stood aside to allow

them to make their way through the gap in the over-grown hedge and up the path to the front door of the disguised Hangar. The place was not visibly changed since the morning. Only the trestle tables were gone. The admiral's rocking chair was still on the veranda. An old lycra jump suit full of holes was draped over the back of the chair. No lights shone in the house. The windows were dark and dusty, but Jack could just see the tatty old lace curtains on the inside. CLt. Jones grabbed the rusty iron knocker on the door and banged it a few times. Jack could hear the echo in the house; it sounded lonely.

"The place sounds empty," cLt. Jones said. "Maybe they've moved out already. This is highly fishy. I'm determined to get to the bottom of it."

"I'll ask the guard," Jack said. He was keen to get back out on the street.

The guard, a Seaman Apprentice from his stripes, turned off his hose when they reached the front gate, saluted again. Even in the dusk it was obvious that watering the defunct flowers was a waste of effort. He nodded to cLt. Jones and said, "If you're thinking of requisitioning this place, ma'am, you'll have to talk to the placement office. No one's lived here for years. It's a bit run down, but I guess a detail that didn't mind a bit of hard work could fix it up."

"We just want to talk to the...officer in charge... about his garage sale."

The Seaman stood with the hose limp in his hand. "Can't really help you, I don't think anyone's planning

a garage sale." He shook his head doubtfully.

Jack said, "There was one this morning. And there was a raffle as well."

"Not here, not next door, not anywhere in this street. Sorry, must have been somewhere else."

Jones looked at him, hard, then at Jack. Jack just shrugged. There didn't seem any point in arguing. "So who used to live here anyway? Floogle says it's the address of Hangar 51."

"Funny old hermit," said the Seaman. He was rolling up the hose neatly and efficiently. "A real loner, the admiral. They said he used to be a famous explorer. He used to go on expeditions collecting wild aliens for zoos. I think he once said something about being the Director at The Other World Zoo. I've no idea where that is—can't be a regular zoo. Some sort of private show, I suppose. But that was years ago. The admiral finally just disappeared. Maybe he went off on one last expedition. I don't know."

"Well, thanks for your help, Seaman," cLt. Jones said. "We'd better be getting back."

"Sure you don't want to requisition the old place

"No, we're leaving for the Academy starship shortly," the cadet Lieutenant said. She caught Jack's eye. "*Not* a word about that to the other cadets, Mr. Wong."

"No ma'am," he said quickly.

The Seaman saluted a final time and marched off briskly into the dusk and around the side of the decrepit building. Jack didn't believe a word of any of it. He was sure that underneath the building the true Hangar

51 stretched downward for many floors, and perhaps outward for many meters or even kilometers. He had a deep suspicion that Hangar 51 was where the scaly, terrifying garage monster had been caged, maybe for many years. But *why*, in the name of all that was holy, he asked himself, head spinning, had the Admiral given it to *Jack?*

∞

When they got back to their quarters and had the flivver retrieved, the domed garage was still slap bang in the middle of the front lawn. Growls and snarls made it vibrate. They went inside and sat down at the mess table. Annie Tan and Rufus Dogge were already seated. An enlisted steward brought them a pot of tea.

"Of course," Annie said, while tea was poured, "you could always raffle the monster alien."

"That's not a bad idea," said Rufus. "It could be a fund-raiser for the unit."

Earlier in the evening cLt. Jones had said she thought there were laws against raffling monster aliens. But now she didn't say anything; maybe, Jack thought, she had changed her mind. Or maybe she was worried about Lt. Zamblott's reaction when he got wind of what had happened while she was the senior cadet officer during his absence.

∞

Lt. Zamblott was back on duty the next day. His leg

had been replaced, and he entered the wardroom with a mug of coffee. From the crabby look on his face, Jack wondered if the mug contained pure lemon juice rather than its usual jolt of rum.

Jack jumped to attention before the Naval officer. "Welcome back, Sir."

"I can't say I missed the place. I quite enjoyed my sick leave. At ease, Wong."

Jack didn't tell him he'd quite enjoyed the holiday from him, too. "Care to buy a ticket in a monster alien raffle, Mr. Zamblott? You could even buy ticket number 001, it's bound to be lucky."

"How much?"

"Twenty yuans, Sir," Jack said.

"Oh well." He pulled a coin from his pocket. "I might as well buy a ticket. There's not a lot you can get for twenty yuans these days."

Jack gave him the ticket. Ten minutes later, Jack followed him into the front office.

"You've won!"

"What have I won?" Lt. Zamblott said. "You never told me what the prize was."

"It's a Monster Garage," Jack said. "You've won a Monster Garage."

"For twenty yuans? I've won a whole garage for twenty yuans?"

"Sure have, Sir. The walls are a bit knocked around— but not too much. It couldn't go to a nicer guy, if you don't mind my saying so. Sir."

"Well, I could certainly do with a garage. Keep the

rain off the flivver."

"We'll arrange to have it brought round to your quarters this afternoon."

"I'm looking forward to seeing it," Zamblott said. You could tell he didn't really believe Jack.

∞

Jack had already discussed how to get the garage to the lucky winner. He told Rufus and Annie about the *We Cart Anything Co.* floater and floogled the firm. A dancing advertisement sang *If it's not nailed down, we can shift it.* Annie used her card and put in their order.

Within minutes, the *We Cart Anything* truck dropped down on the lawn. A large woman was fixing the chains from the crane to the dome of the garage.

"Good day," she said.

"How's it going?" Jack said.

"Fine," she said. "You didn't keep this baby long. We only delivered it to you yesterday."

"A mix up," Jack said. "It's the wrong size."

"Never mind," the woman said. "The new owner will like it."

"He sure will," Jack said.

She stood back from the garage and pressed a button. The floater's engine purred into life and the chains began to tighten. Slowly the garage began to leave the ground. It swayed slightly. Wild roaring ensued. Jack had been expecting this—he had not expected the monster alien to enjoy being moved again. He felt a spurt of sympathy of the creature. Poor thing. It wasn't

anything like the five legged monsters who had imprisoned him for more than a week in the stinky heat. In
fact, the monster's plight was rather like his own had
been.

"What's that!" yelled the crane woman, surprised
and alarmed.

"It's just the monster alien," Jack said. "Don't worry
about it."

"What monster alien?"

"It must have made the same sort of racket yesterday,"
Jack said.

"There was nothing in the garage yesterday," the
woman said. "What the hell's going on?"

The monster alien screamed again and started
banging the sides of the garage.

"I'm not sure we can shift this," she yelled above the
racket. "There's health and safety issues here. We're
talking hazardous cargo."

"You can shift anything," Jack yelled. "It's not nailed
down."

"It sure as hell *ought* to be nailed down."

"Keep lifting," Jack said. "The sooner you get it on
the floater, the better."

But the crane chain had stopped. The garage was
swaying. It swung and lurched half a meter from the
ground. The monster alien was giving the walls a
hammering—screeching and snarling. Jack noticed
something that really frightened him. The garage had
no floor. The monster alien was standing on the front
lawn. Below the base of the curving wall, Jack could

see great scaled paws ripping at the grass. A pale, mutilated rose blossom was flung out.

"Put it *down*," Jack yelled.

"Right," shouted the woman, so spooked that she jabbed the button for the warning horn, provoking an enraged scream from the monster.

The sudden silence that followed was worse than the roaring and hammering. There was now a gap below the bottom of the garage perimeter. Jack watched two immense alien paws probing. Suddenly there were four paws. The monster alien was crouching. Then its face was suddenly snarling at them. Its teeth were like broken piano keys.

"Jesus. *Run*," yelled the woman.

Jack was about to do just that. Before he could move, the monster alien shoved its way through the gap. At the same moment, the woman pressed another button and lowered the garage with a jolt. The monster alien was suddenly trapped, half in, half out of the garage. It snarled and heaved—and the whole garage rose up into the air. The monster alien was out, standing on the lawn. Jack was too terrified to run. So was the woman. The control slate dropped from her fingers. The monster alien stood up straight, looked at them, and grinned.

∞

Jack hadn't been expecting a grin. He stood staring at the monster alien. It looked quite pleased with itself. No more roars and screams. It used its great scaly

paws to brush itself down, then shrugged. "Pah!" it said. "Think your nasty little shed can keep a warrior Xlaquat in prison, do you?" Its accent was surprisingly refined. "Well, think again, you turkeys."

The monster alien, the warrior Xlaquat, strolled out into the street and strode away. Cool as a cucumber.

"Well, blow me down," said the removalist. She bent to retrieve her slate, and her hand was still shaking a little. "I've never seen one of those Xlaquats before. What was it?"

"No idea," Jack said. His own jaw was trembling with the aftershock. "Would you like a cup of tea or something?"

"I guess I need something, if you know what I mean," the woman said.

∞

By the time the rest of the Company returned from their revels, Jack had given the woman a cup of coffee heavily laced with rum, and some cookies and convinced her that it was now appropriate to take the empty garage round to Lt. Zamblott's billet. Jack was sad to see it go. Still, Lt. Zamblott had won it fair and square in a raffle. Jack had to let him keep it.

Hortense Jones was pleased that the garage had disappeared, but none of the other cadets were thrilled about the monster alien wandering off.

"We should call the police," Annie Tan said.

"They'd just think we were cranks," Suzy Mugabe said. "Who ever heard of a monster alien suddenly

appearing on Earth and just walking away?"

"Well, it happened. We know it happened."

"Oh, garbage."

"We should have taken pictures," Rufus said.

"That wouldn't have helped much," Jack said. "There's nothing you can't do with vids. The cops would just think we'd rendered the monster alien as a prank."

"Anyway," Annie said, "if it's just wandering around the neighborhood someone else will call the police. They'll get dozens of calls."

"Bet you the monster alien is already on the news feeds."

They floogled up the news, holding their breath. Nothing. No mention of a monster warrior Xlaquat. Jack felt a sharp sting of disappointment; surely a real live monster alien loose on a military base was news.

Rufus Dogge shut off the feed and said, "I don't understand how the alien got into the garage in the first place. That delivery person insisted the garage was empty, and anyway it didn't have a floor."

"Unless the warrior Xlaquat *chewed it up.*"

"The Rear Admiral must have brought it round from Hangar 51" Jack said. "It was his monster alien. Maybe it just walked round with him. Like a dog. Maybe it was on a lead."

"People would have stared. Anyway, it could talk. Way smarter than a dog."

"I doubt that that would have worried Admiral Martinique," Jack said. "Maybe the monster alien went

right back home to Wilson Street, maybe that's why it wasn't in the news."

"Well, we're not going back to Wilson Street to find out," Jones said.

∞

Three days later Jack got back from the immersion center, where he'd been boning up on interstellar diplomacy tactics, and made coffee. He took it out into the back garden and nearly dropped the cup. The monster alien was back, sitting under the Tesla power array coils. The warrior Xlaquat glanced up, hearing Jack's moan, and saw him, but failed to scream and rage. The alien just looked oddly composed. Jack felt no impulse to engage it in conversation. He dashed back inside and bolted the door. He went into the kitchen and looked out of the window. The monster alien still sat under the Tesla array, its scales glimmering in the faint discharge. It looked thinner than Jack remembered. Jack suspected it had not been getting enough sustenance. That made him shudder. The thing could prefer a diet of *anything*—garage flooring or human flesh, who knew?

He heard the front door clang open; from the clatter, cLt. Julia Durango.

"Shut the door, Ma'am," Jack yelled. "Lock it. Come and look at this."

Durango surged into the kitchen. "What are you blathering on about, Wong? Lock the door? Are we in a siege-type situation here?"

"I dunno," Jack said. "Have a look under the Tesla coil."

"Hell," said Durango, "it's him. The alien warrior. He's come back. Cool."

"He doesn't look all that fierce for a warrior," Jack said.

"I'd say he's hungry," Durango said.

"So what are we going to feed him, live goats?"

"He might be a vegan, Let's give him a gannyapple."

"I'm not going anywhere near him, are you crazy?"

"We'll throw it to him, Wong."

Durango found a Ganymede apple and irised the back door a fraction, just enough for a peep. Jack followed, staying right behind her. If the warrior Xlaquat charged, Jack was going to grab his Company mate by the back of her jump suit, much as he hated her 'holier than thou' attitude about her superior cadet rank, and pull her smartly into the house before winking the door shut.

Durango opened the door a little wider and yelled, "Hey, monster alien, buddy. Wanna apple?"

The monster alien regarded them cooly. She pitched the fruit. It sailed through the air like a baseball. The monster alien took the catch with ease. He looked at the gannyapple, polished it on his scaly pelt, leaving scraps of puce peel, and ate it in three chomps. He studied their faces through the partly open door. The expression on his face said it all, but the Xlaquat opened his frightful mouth and said it anyway: "Thank you, human infantas. I'd relish another one or two of those."

"Get him another one, Wong," Durango said.

"Okay, but let's shut the door first," Jack said.

"No," she said, and gave him a contemptuous glare. "You scared, you pussy? That would look unwelcoming. Go and get an apple."

Jack fetched another two gannyapples and tossed one to the monster alien. This time the Xlaquat caught it one handed—just stuck out his paw and speared the apple with a single claw. Three chomps and it was gone.

They fed the monster alien six apples, four bananas, a lettuce, two zucchini and two bowls of shark flakes. The first bowl Jack left on the back veranda and scuttled back inside. They watched from the kitchen window as the monster alien got to his feet and strode over to the shark flakes. He picked up the bowl, opened his mouth and poured the flakes down his throat without having to swallow. The Xlaquat brought the empty bowl to the window, held it out. He was only a meter away from them on the other side of the hardened glass. The look on his face said, *More?*

Heart thumping Jack opened the window and the alien handed back the bowl. For a second, hand touched paw. The alien's scales felt sharp yet strangely benign, unthreatening. Jack refilled the bowl with shark flakes and handed it back. Again the creature tipped it straight down his throat, passed back the bowl, belched, said, "Thank you," gave Jack back the bowl, strolled over to the Tesla array, lay down on the grass and went to sleep.

"Quite friendly," Jack said, pulse slowing. "I always

thought so. He even talks our language."

"Then why was he kicking up such a fuss the other day?"

"He just doesn't like being locked up. Would you? I'd throw a fit if someone locked me in a garage."

"Well, he can't stay in the back garden."

"Oh, I don't know," Jack said. "I guess he'd make a really nice mascot."

∞

"Not on my watch, cadet Ensign!" said cLt. Jones—a comment Jack promptly ignored.

The few cadet Lieutenants in the know took some persuading not to call the police, the zoo, the council ranger, the Department of Alien Environments, or all of the above. But in the end, Jack convinced them to let the monster alien stay for a few days.

"And I mean *a few days*," said cLt Jones. "We can't keep feeding that alien, it's against regulations. Anyway, it's probably unsanitary."

"We'd better give him a name," cLt Durango said.

"He's already got a name," cadet Ensign Annie Tan said. "I mean, he can talk. Why don't we ask him?"

"He's an alien on our planet," said Durango. "He can use a human name or go back where he came from."

"What about Wilson?" Jack said. "He comes from Wilson Street."

"Good as any," Rufus said.

Wilson the monster alien warrior Xlaquat took up residence in the back garden. Jack taught him how to

hold a baseball bat. When he hit the ball it disappeared in the general direction of the South Pole. The cadets were only permitted to use a tennis ball off the sports field, so Jack figured it probably didn't do any damage. Wilson tried to help them do some weeding, but he couldn't distinguish a weed from a flower. Jack told him to just sit and watch. Wilson did something terrifying with his teeth that was either a throttled roar or the equivalent of a shrug, but he didn't pull anything else out of the ground. But while it was all very well having a pet monster alien in the back garden, Jack wanted to take him out, show him off.

As the Company were watching a game on the image window in the wardroom, yelling at it and swigging beers, Jack had a good idea. In the warm-up before the start of a game, the home team's mascot, a guy dressed up in a furry alien suit, cavorted with the boy and girl cheerleaders. He'd dance around, grab-assing and tumbling, getting the crowd into a good mood. Here was the way to make Wilson acceptable to the general public—disguise him as the sort of mascot he resembled. If people supposed an ordinary human was inside a scaly suit, he'd be fine.

The thing to do for major retro appeal was to give him a sandwich board, with shoulder straps and advertisements on back and front. Jack found two large flex flatscreens and made a pair of shoulder straps out of a sagging brassiere he'd located in the recycle dumpster behind the women's bachelor officers' quarters. But what message? Jack pondered. Maybe it was true

that the Rear Admiral has been the Director at The Other World Zoo. Perfect! A simple advertisement: *Visit the Other World Zoo.* Jack rendered it in bright red and yellow flashers. It was brilliantly professional, he decided.

After lunch on Saturday, Jack took the contraption out to Wilson. The alien didn't resist as he drew the sandwich board over the Xlaquat's head and clipped the strap tight, apparently regarding it as a fashion accessory. He strutted around the garden like a model on a catwalk.

"Come on, Wilson," Jack said. "We'll go for a walk downtown."

"My name is Tharam," the Xlaquat muttered darkly, but Jack was too excited to pay any attention.

∞

At the shopping mall, people gazed at Wilson without surprise. Just a guy dressed up in a silly suit doing a bit of advertising. Jack and Wilson window shopped, met up with Ensign Suzy Mugabe and Rufus Rupert Trevor Dogge and a couple of other cadets from the Company.

"Who's your friend?" Suzy Mugabe said with a grin.

"Wilson," Jack said.

Wilson waved his great scaly arms around in a friendly manner.

"It must be pretty hot inside that suit," a passing shopper said.

"Oh, Wilson is used to it," Jack said. "He's done a lot

of this sort of work."

"Can't he talk for himself?"

"Not very well. The suit is pretty thick."

"Let's get a slurpy," Suzy said.

"Good idea," Jack said. And then he realized it wasn't a very good idea at all. He'd have to get a slurpy for Wilson as well. Jack knew only too well what Wilson would do with it. "Actually it wouldn't be fair to Wilson," he said, "He's not allowed to eat or drink on duty."

"Oh get real," Suzy said. "Of course he can have a slurpy." She turned to the alien. "You'd like one, wouldn't you, Wilson?" She gestured towards the Hot Donut shop.

Wilson's eyes followed Suzy's gesture. He saw the glass counter with the donuts and pastries underneath, he saw the pictures of a hundred drinks on the back wall. He saw the chairs and tables, the happy customers eating donuts and drinking slurpies and set off at a trot towards the Hot Donut. Jack followed close on his heels. They reached a vacant table. "Sit down!" Easier said than done if you are wearing a flexing sandwich board, but Wilson managed well enough, fitting the back of the sandwich board over the chair.

Jack punched in an order for slurpies. A willowy Centaurian waitress arrived with a tray of slurpies in cardboard drink containers with straws. As she put the tray down on the table, Wilson reached out an immense scaled paw, grabbed a slurpy, tilted back his head, opened his mouth as wide as was possible

and dropped the slurpy in. With a mighty gulp and a swallow he consumed the lot: drink, cardboard, straw.

"Gross!" yelled Suzy Mugabe.

The waitress screamed and jumped back. She pointed wildly at Wilson. "That's...that's...that's not a man in a suit. That's a monster alien."

"He's quite tame," Jack said.

Things went dangerously quiet. Everybody in the mall seemed to be looking at them. Wilson looked around. He saw everybody staring and put on a show. He reached out and grabbed another slurpy. It went down the hatch as fast as the first. He grabbed a donut and threw it high into the air. It fell straight into his huge open mouth with the teeth like piano keys. Wilson let out a huge belch and tried to rub his abdomen. But he was wearing the sandwich board, so instead he ended up banging the flexscreen like a drum. The bra strap twanged, flinging the screens up and down as if Wilson was attempting flight..

"Call the constables," the waitress yelled.

Half a dozen people started punching in the 000 number. Others screamed and ran.

"Come on, Wilson," Jack said. "We're out of here."

The alien seemed reluctant to leave.

"He wants another slurpy," Suzy said.

"I'll buy him two," Jack told him. "Later."

Jack grabbed a scaly arm, rasping the skin of his palm, and tried to pull Wilson to his feet. "Come on, chief," Jack said. "Before the cops and the dog-catcher arrive."

They ran out of the mall, shoppers scattering in front of them. Once outside, Wilson set off at a steady jog, saying nothing but at least not roaring. Jack jogged along behind him. The warrior Xlaquat seemed to know exactly where he was going. He turned corners and ducked down little lanes like someone who had grown up in the district, which seemed grossly unlikely, or perhaps like an alien spy who had studied Floogle Earth with ferocious diligence. Police sirens shrilled in the distance.

After ten minutes of jogging, Jack was tired, out of breath, and also lost. He had never been in this particular district before. Wilson, tireless, jogged along beside a high brick wall. Jack was gasping for breath. Wilson stopped suddenly; Jack ran into him, slammed his nose on the iron back. He cursed feebly. They stood at a rusty turnstile gate in the middle of the brick wall. An ancient turnstiles with bars, the sort where you can go in, but you can't go out. A sign beside the turnstile read *The Amazing Other World Zoo—Free Entry— See the aliens do tricks.*

The Rear Admiral from Hangar 51 had collected animals for something called *The Other World Zoo,* allegedly. Probably he had collected Wilson for this very zoo, from some distant godforsaken planet outside the limits of the Earth Imperium. Breathing hard, Jack listened, and drew in air through his itching nostrils. The place certainly sounded and stank like a zoo, he could hear hooting and the odd roar. Lions, maybe, or

something far more disturbing.

But free entry? There must be some catch. Jack had no time to find out. Wilson grabbed hold of him, pushed him through the turnstile, followed like a force of nature in the next quarter of the stile. It creaked a bit, turning, and the warrior Xlaquat was almost trapped as it went round when the sandwich boards jammed in the works. His chest swelled, and a growl emerged. The machinery was rusty; it gave way with a screech and a clang.

∞

The sign was right and wrong. It was right about the *Free Entry*: nobody asked them for money. In fact nobody was around to ask for money. The place was deserted. But the sign was wrong about the zoo being amazing. It wasn't remotely amazing. In fact, the whole place looked tacky and run down, as decrepit as 27 Wilson Street. Maybe that was a clue. If Wilson St. hid the marvels of Hangar 51, who knew what astonishments lurked inside *The Amazing Other World Zoo?*

A narrow path twisted its way between ample cages of odd looking monkeys, if that's what they were, and implausible parrots with four wings apiece. Jack trudged after Wilson, who seemed right at home. Had he, indeed, once lived in this zoo? Maybe the Rear Admiral had brought him home as a pet. That was against Imperial policy, of course. Lesser species were meant to be guided on the upward path of civilization, firmly if necessary, but never maltreated. Although

you'd have to be pretty stupid to mistreat a warrior Xlaquat, it looked like. Jack shivered.

Wilson was strolling down the path, smirking at the monkeys and parrots, as if to say, "Hello again, my comrades." The aliens just stared at them as they went by. Jack was irritated. Neither the monkey things nor the quasi-parrots were doing tricks. The sign had been wrong about that as well.

They wandered on, Jack in a kind of daze, just looking at the aliens. The air smelled odd, and not just from *eau d'excrément*. The farther they walked the more the captive creatures looked like beasts from unknown planets. A sad wolf paced up and down, but it wasn't a wolf. It had a goat's face, topped with green spiral horns. As they passed its cage the alien creature stopped in its tracks and glared at them with eyes like pale marbles. Wilson stared back silently for a moment at the goat-wolf. Maybe they knew each other, but if so they weren't friends.

∞

The path branched. They went left, stood for a while looking at a cage full of green rabbits the size of ponies, ears on backwards. At another turning they found themselves between a cage of scaly otters and a pool of aquatic animals like penguins with gauzy fairy wings. The otters stood on their hind legs and all slowly turned their heads as Jack walked by. You'd think they'd never seen a human before, or a monster alien.

An hour passed, or longer. Jack was surprised at how big the zoo was, much larger than he'd first thought. They had been wandering along for kilometers. He felt dizzy, almost hallucinatory. And he was getting sick of the place. Why had Wilson brought him here? His stomach cramped in a moment of pure dread. Was the alien monster planning to trap him, leave him penned in one of these cages? He stared about, looking for the exit. He couldn't find a turnstile, couldn't even work out where the entrance turnstile had been located. The sky was blurred with opalescent clouds. He knew that if he followed the sun he could make sense of the geography, but the sun was lost behind a sky of light. My god, he thought, am I even on Earth any longer?

Jack tugged at Wilson' arm,

"How do we get out of here?"

Wilson just shrugged.

Things were getting crazy. Jack kept taking turnings and going back on his tracks. Wilson tagged along. Sometimes they were in a new stretch of the zoo, sometimes Jack was in a place he seemed to recognize. The zoo seemed to stretch for kilometers in all directions. The sky was changing color but not in a standard setting sun way. The aliens were giving him the creeps. He began to focus his attention on a search for somebody who could give him directions. There wasn't anybody. Jack was the only human in the place. His flesh crawled with a horrid suspicion.

"Am I dead, Wilson? Is this some sort of shitty afterlife?"

The monster alien regarded him with a kind of bleak amusement.

But then somehow they were back at the fairy penguin pond. An old zoo keeper in a billed cap was throwing fish from a bucket. Jack leaned on the rail that ran along the top of the low wall and watched for a few minutes. At last he was getting a bit of action. The penguins were zooming through the water like little torpedoes, then leaping up and sailing through the air on extended wings. The keeper glanced at them, raising his head, and said, "Hello, Fang, come back have you?" It was Rear Admiral Ricardo Fortesque Martinique (ret.).

Wilson snarled at the man and let out a frightful roar. He was just like the old Wilson from the garage raffle. But the keeper, the admiral, the Director of the Zoo, only shrugged, then turned to Jack.

"Good afternoon, young feller," he said. "A nice day for a maze."

"For a what?" Jack said.

"A maze," said the admiral. "Didn't you read the sign? This is a mazing zoo."

Jack groaned. It wasn't a very funny joke, although the layout of the zoo had certainly been nightmarish and confusing. "Look," Jack said. "Let's get this straight, Admiral Martinique. You're saying the zoo has been designed as a maze?"

"Surely has."

"So how do we get out?"

"Out?" said the admiral. "Out? You want to get out?"

"Of course."

The admiral scratched his head and looked at him as if Jack were the unstable one. "I've never heard of anybody getting out," he said at last. "That's what the aliens do. The aliens get out, but we can't have the people doing that as well."

"What? Why not?"

"Well, it wouldn't be right, would it? We've got to keep the people and the aliens separate. That's why we have bars and moats. Not that they stopped your friend Fang."

"His name's Wilson," Jack said.

"Tharam," said the warrior Xlaquat in a rough, deep, threatening voice.

"Suit yourselves," said the admiral.

The old boy was clearly nuts. Jack wasn't going to get any sense out of him. And now the penguins were kicking up a fuss, flapping their ridiculous wings, demanding the last of the fish. Jack left the admiral to it.

Another human, a smartly dressed woman with a handbag, was on the point of disappearing around a corner. Jack ran after her, caught up with her outside a cage full of liar birds snarling and disputing. Fang or Wilson or Tharam or whatever his name was paced at his heels.

"Hey," Jack said. "Which way to the exit?"

"I don't know," she said crossly. "I've been looking for it for hours myself." She looked at Wilson's tattered, flickering sandwich board. "*Visit the Zoo*, indeed!

That's the worst advice you could give anybody. I think I'll call the police." She pulled a phone from her handbag, jammed it in her ear, punched some numbers. She tapped her foot impatiently. "Oh, hello. Is that the police…? I'd like to be rescued. I'm stuck in a zoo.... What do you mean—'That's the best place for you'…? Look, to whom am I speaking? Sgt. Diprotodon? Is this mean to be a joke, Sergeant…? Really! I'll complain to your superiors…! I've never been so insulted…I want to know the name of your watch commander…? Captain Gonococcus!" The woman snapped the phone from her ear and stuffed it back in her handbag. "Well, really!" she said.

A pair of ancient pensioners shuffled up.

"I am telling you, Bandhura," the old gentleman was saying to his wife, "I am not liking the way these animals are looking at us. I am not relishing their attitude."

"They are aliens, not just animals, Gopichand."

"They seem to think they are having the right to stare at us. Just look at that brute."

The old fellow pointed his walking stick at a feathered ape standing at the front of her cage looking sardonically at them. The ape picked up a stick from the floor of its cage and pointed at the old guy. Gopichand shook his walking stick at the ape. The ape shook her stick at Gopichand.

Jack grinned and thumbed his nose at the ape. The ape thumbed her flat nose back. Jack pretended to drag his knuckles along the ground. The ape sneered,

showing all her enormous grinding teeth, and shoved one spatulate thumb into an ear, pretending to yak into a phone.

"Well, really!" said the phone woman.

Other apes approached from the back of the cage and stood in line looking at the humans. They pointed and pulled faces of disgust. One ape held a plastic bag full of peanuts. It shared out the peanuts with the other apes. When they each had a handful, they began to hurl the peanuts through the bars of their cage. Several landed in the phone woman's hair. She brushed them off and stamped on them in a rage.

"I wouldn't waste good food if I were you," a voice said behind us. The humans and Wilson turned and looked into the liar birds' cage. The old admiral was there, pouring out a bucket of bird seed for the squabbling prevaricators.

"Moldy peanuts aren't what I'd call 'good food'," the woman said. "Not after they've been handled by an ape with feathers."

"What else are you going to eat?" said the admiral. "The penguin fairies might let you have some raw fish. But then they mightn't. They're hungry birds, those penguins."

"Raw fish!" said the woman. "We are not in one of the Nipponese colonies, I trust. I believe you had better tell us where the exit is, and quickly or it will be the worse for you, sir."

"The only exit I know about is for the aliens," the admiral said. "You wouldn't want to use that exit."

"Well, really," said the woman.

Wilson and Jack left the humans muttering among themselves and made one last attempt to find a way out. Jack gave himself an hour to find the exit. If he couldn't find it, then he would have to climb out—find the outside wall of the maze and clamber over it somehow. Maybe Wilson could help him. Fang, whatever. The alien warrior could come too—or, if he felt happier inside, stay behind in the zoo.

Now they were walking fast down a path between peacock cages, keeping an eye on the setting sun. Or was it rising? If it was setting, at least Jack knew where west was. Or east. Or if they weren't on Earth anymore, who could guess? At the very least, he could stop himself going round and round in circles. If he persisted in a straight line he would have to reach the outside wall eventually. Unfortunately, none of the paths ran in straight lines. Above his head a voice shrieked, "No exit! No exit! No exit!"

Jack looked up, startled, couldn't see anybody.

"No exit! No exit! No exit!"

A sulfur-crested cockatoo was screeching, except its crest wasn't sulfur-yellow, it was lurid purple, and its feet were rings of tentacle. The cocky wasn't in a cage. Cockies, Jack told himself, half-delirious, are a sort of parrot. They can learn to mimic speech, they just don't know what they are saying. But still, in this weird zoo anything might happen. Feeling like a fool, he tried to talk sensibly to the cockatoo thing.

"There's got to be an exit," Jack said.

"No way, buster! No way, buster! No way, buster!"

"No need to say everything three times," Jack said crossly. He felt at the end of his tether.

"Twice is nice! Twice is nice!"

"Once will do," Jack said.

"Boring!" screamed the cocky.

"Yeah, all right," Jack said. Had the alien cocky actually understood him? Maybe it had just learnt to say these things without knowing what the words meant. Jack decided to give it a little test. "What's two and two?" Jack said.

"Forty-four! Forty-four! Forty-four!"

"Rubbish!"

"Half eight!"

"Hey...that's right," Jack said. "Very good."

"Pieces of eight! Pieces of eight! Pieces of eight!" shouted the cocky.

"What are pieces of eight?" Jack said.

"I don't know," said the cocky, "It's just what we parrots always say. We also always want a cracker. We shout: Polly wants a cracker, Polly wants a cracker, Polly wants a cracker. It's the done thing."

"So you *can* understand me?"

"I'm not stupid! I'm not stupid! I'm not...."

"All right, all right," Jack yelled, "Just tell me how to get out of here."

"There's no need to repeat yourself," said the bird.

"I didn't—"

"You did so too. You said 'All right' twice. I heard you perfectly well the first time."

"Look, buster," Jack said, "cut the cackle. Just tell me—"

"Cackle!" screamed the cocky, outraged. "I'm not a hen! Not a fowl! Not a pullet!"

"I don't care. Just tell me how to get out of this goddam zoo."

"Fly! Fly! Fly!— That's how I get out."

"I'm not a bird," Jack said.

"The penguins aren't much of a bird either," said the cocky. "Mostly they fly under water. Talk about stupid! Talk about stupid!"

"So I'm meant to *swim* out of this zoo, like a fairy penguin?"

"The stupid penguins are your only hope," said the bird. "Only hope! Only hope!"

"How come?" Jack said.

"No bars! No bars! No bars!"

Jack puckered his forehead, thought for a moment. "You're right."

"I'm right! I'm right! I'm right!" screamed the cockatoo and its purple crest stood up. The setting sun made it look like a small firework blazing out of its head. Yes, definitely sunset, it was getting lower in the sky, nearing the horizon. But which world? The loquacious bird spread its huge white wings and flapped away. As it disappeared Jack heard it screeching, "Pieces of eight! Pieces of eight! Pieces of eight!"

∞

The bird had been right; no bars rose around the

penguin fairies' enclosure. All the other animals' enclosures were separated from the public by heavy barriers. There was no way the animals and humans could get into each others' space. But now Jack considered the matter, all there was between the fairies' pond and the humans was a low wall with a railing on the top. He set off, desperately trying to find his way back to the penguins. Wilson jogged along beside him, saying nothing as usual.

It must have been about five o'clock when the aliens stopped staring at them as they jogged past. The creatures all crowded around the doors at the backs of their cages. Suddenly a hooter sounded. The zoo was closing. Jack heard the clicks of doors being centrally unlocked and the admiral yelling at the aliens. "Don't all rush at once," he shouted. "Easy does it."

Jack saw where he was, back in familiar territory where the feathered apes had been housed. But their cage was empty now. Jack shot round to the fairies' enclosure, passing more empty cages. Wilson loped beside him like a dinosaur from prehistory. Jack turned to him,

"You coming too, then?"

Wilson just shrugged. Jack took a good grip on the rail on the low wall, hauled himself up and over, landed in the fairies' pool. Wilson splashed loudly down beside him. The water was up to their waists, but Jack was past worrying about soaked shoes and clothing. He waded to the other side, climbed some rocks, was through the open door in a flash. Wilson followed.

They stood in a narrow lane running behind the backs of cages. Jack hoped desperately that the alien menagerie were already well clear of the place. They dashed down the lane, Jack breathing hard, passing a couple of spiny things shuffling along like snails.

They fetched up at a turnstile in a high brick wall. Without a pause they were through the turnstile and out into the street. It was the same street they had entered by. Or was it? The bark on some of the trees had been chewed by beavers or some similar creature. He hadn't noticed that before. Jack looked up into the branches. There were blue-skinned beings with six limbs and no heads swinging lithely about, utterly at home. A car went by with a sudden screech. It wasn't brakes. It was the shriek of a parrot. The car was full of aliens, including the parrot. It was being driven by something that looked like a heavily maned lion. Jack took no notice. He was staring at the sign by the turnstile in the fence. It read: *The Amazing Other World Zoo—$5 Entry. Kittens, puppies and cubs, half price.—See the humans do tricks.*

∞

"Oh my god," Jack said to Wilson. "We're in another world. An other world. We are on some sort of alien planet. You see this sort of thing in sims. People go through the backs of wardrobes. They fall through wormholes in space. That happened to me not long ago, actually." He started to shake, and couldn't stop. His teeth rattled together as his jaw tremored. "They

go through mirrors and down rabbit holes. They visit other worlds in their dreams. It's not meant to actually *happen*."

Wilson shrugged. Jack wasn't sure about Wilson, maybe he found it beneath his dignity to speak in a human language. "How about you take that sandwich board off?" Jack said. Wilson shrugged again, but he removed the sandwich board and propped it against the wall. "Well, at least it's in the right place," Jack said. "It says *Visit the Zoo.*"

Wilson scratched himself and grimaced. Or was that a grin?

"Now look, Wilson," Jack said slowly and clearly. "You've got to get me out of here. Understand? I want to go home, back to my own world. Savvy?"

"Very well." Wilson beckoned, started to walk away. Jack went after him, exhausted and dispirited. If he was stuck on some mad world full of aliens, the warrior Xlaquat was his only friend. He quickened his pace. No letting him out of his sight.

The street looked reasonably conventional, but the houses had unusual doors. Some were huge (for elephants? woolly mammoths? dinosaurs?). Many doors looked so small that a human couldn't fit through them. A couple of four legged creatures that looked a bit like starving antelopes with immense wings landed on the sidewalk ahead of them, pranced away down a side street. Jack was dizzy again, having difficulty believing what he saw.

They came to a street of shops. One bore a faded

picture painted on its front window: a huge winged cat flying across a sky filled with stars and planets with rings. Once that sky must have been brilliant; now the gold and silver was peeling or absent. A sign flickered: *The Great Flapping Cat Café*. As cafés ran, this one was pretty run down.

Before they entered, the warrior Xlaquat paused and scratched his belly again. Jack felt his gorge rise; the creature's claw delved *inside* that expanse of scales, drew something out into the fading light. Jack gave a shaky laugh. Wilson had been wearing an environment suit this whole time! A clawed hand extended, held out the thing he had just removed from the pocket. It was a small wrinkled seed.

"What's this?"

"My gift to you, Jack Wong. It is a cow seed. Look after it, and when the moment is opportune, plant it in a bowl of milk. You will be glad you did."

Speechless, and strangely moved, Jack took the seed and placed it carefully in his belt pouch. A *cow* seed?

Wilson gave the door a shove and they went inside. The café was dimly lit and smelled rank: food, but animal or alien food. The floor was covered in straw. A barnyard of alien creatures sat at tables, eating, drinking and making merry. The room roared with animal noise: barking, snuffling, cackling, hooting, yowling. At one table a group of dogs, feathered apes, octopuses in water suits and other beings were playing cards. Some had real hands or tentacles with which to hold the cards. The rest were making do, not very well,

with trotters and paws. Two of the animals were human. One was the Rear Admiral, his jumpsuit even more torn and gappy, so that his veiny, wrinkled, pale flesh showed through. The other human was Lt. Zamblott.

"Mr. Zamblott, Sir!" Jack cried. "What are you doing here?"

"A fine mess you've got me into, Wong," he said.

"Me?" Jack said.

"Yes, you. You and your damn monster garage."

"The garage?"

"Yeah, I'd been parking my flivver in it for a week before I noticed a little door at the back under the window. When I crawled through the door I came out in another world. This world! It's a madhouse. And I've been stuck here for more than three years, waiting for you to arrive."

Three *years?* Obviously he meant three hours. Either that or he'd flipped his wig.

"I will admit that this future civilization does take some getting used to," said Rear Admiral Ricardo Fortesque Martinique (ret.). "But you'll settle in...."

"The hell we will," Jack said. "Me and Lt. Zamblott want to go home. Now. Sir."

"This civilization of galactic equals has certain advantages," said the admiral. "It might seem strange at first—"

"Forget the advantages," Jack shouted. The dining room lapsed into silence. Aliens of every kind stared reproachfully at them. "We want out."

"Sir."

"Sir, yes, Sir."

"Ah, my young friend, have you no sense of adventure?"

"No, Sir. I had enough adventure last year when a bunch of five-legged aliens tried to, to *worship* me." He shook his head. "No, it was worse than that. To worship my suit's Machiavellian intelligence. They treated me like an *animal*." For days, he'd feared he was marooned for the rest of his life—trapped on a hot, steamy, unknown world with mad aliens who wouldn't let him go.

"The youth of today!" said the old officer sadly. "Young people were different in my day. But listen to me, Jack Wong. Why do you suppose I led you step by step to this place and time? Why do you imagine human-grade AIs are banned from Earth?"

"What?"

"The universe is a very much larger and stranger place than you imagine, young man." The hubbub was rising again as the alien creatures, bored by the spectacle of nothing better than a lecture to an irritated young human, went back to their plates and troughs. "Your pod went through a wormhole anomaly and was displaced in space. But there are more complex folds in spacetime. Some can take you into—"

"How do we get out of here?" Jack said, interrupting the old fool.

The admiral sighed, and exchanged a weary glance with Zamblott. "What would you expect to find in a boat shed?"

"We've been through this before, Sir," Jack said.

"And a hay barn, a tram depot, a tool shed...."

"Yeah, yeah," Jack said. "All of the above."

"And what would you expect to find in the Great Flapping Cat Café?"

"A great cat flap," Jack snapped. He was getting totally sick of silly word games.

"And what do you see there?" said the admiral, pointing at the door Jack and Wilson had just come through.

Wearily, Jack looked over his shoulder. Sure enough, there was a cat flap at the bottom of the door. But it was a lot bigger than usual; a lion or tiger could have squeezed through it. Jack groaned again at the pun. They do call lions and tigers *the great cats*.

"I so hope this works," Jack told the aged admiral. He turned to Lt. Zamblott. "After you, Sir."

"After you," the lieutenant said.

"No, no, Sir," Jack said. "Please, you go first. I want to say good bye to my pal Wilson."

"Very well, then," said Lt. Zamblott. He crossed to the door and got down on his hands and knees and started to crawl through the cat flap. He got stuck. His butt was just a bit too wide.

Jack turned to Wilson, "Do the right thing," he said.

Wilson knew what to do, all right. He put one scaly foot, claws carefully retracted, on Lt. Zamblott's buttocks and gave a shove. The lieutenant disappeared with a pop into the past. The cat flap clanged shut. Now it was Jack's turn.

"Goodbye, Wilson," Jack said. "It's been good to know you."

Wilson put his huge rough arm round Jack's shoulders and squeezed.

"Tharam," he said.

"I'm sorry, I see, Tharam. I didn't realize you meant that was your name. I'm a bit thick sometimes. You've probably noticed."

"Farewell, Jack Wong. And don't lose that seed."

Jack didn't look back, he was down on his hands and knees and through the cat flap in seconds. He stood up outside the Hot Donut in the shopping mall. Lt. Zamblott was there as well, brushing a dirty footprint from his backside and glaring at Jack.

"Uh, Wilson did that, Sir!"

"You and your garages," said the lieutenant.

Jack looked around. It was just an ordinary late afternoon in the mall. Shopkeepers were getting ready to close. The flower shop attendant was taking the buckets of ordinary flowers out to the cool room. A notice in the window of the pet shop offered two sets of clones for the price of one.

"See you back at the Company tomorrow morning, Sir," Jack said to Lt. Zamblott.

"I suppose so," he said. He didn't sound very enthusiastic.

"Look," Jack said. "If you don't like being an instructor, you can always go back to the future and live with the aliens. I mean, you're the owner of the Monster Garage, Sir. Just duck through the little door

at the back, any time you like."

"Watch it, Wong. Besides, I don't think I'll be keeping that garage. Thinking of running a little raffle, actually. You wouldn't like to buy a ticket, would you?"

"No, Sir, but thank you," Jack said. He pushed his hand into his pocket and touched the seed he'd been given. He couldn't wait to plant it.

CHAPTER THREE
SKYHOOK

"Give me two burgers with the lot and a shot of rye," Jack Wong said. He sat deep inside the Space Academy starship, watching the wall screen in his cabin. The Academy was moving smoothly onto orbit around a tiny moon barely larger than the starship, high above the equator of Bargleplod.

"Please," said the soft voice behind him.

"Please what?"

"You mean, 'Give me two burgers with the lot and a shot of rye, *please*,'" the voice said.

Jack turned and looked at the cow.

"Give me a break," he said. "You're just as annoying as the Mac." He still shuddered at the memory.

"You are a very rude young man," the cow told him. It settled down on its back legs, two pistons that looked like gleaming anti-gravitino pumps.

"You're just a machine," Jack said, turning back to the image on the screen.

Bargleplod was so large you couldn't really see that it was a globe. It looked like a huge round billboard hanging against the starry blackness of space,

smeared with red and yellow and orange stripes. Jack couldn't keep his eyes off the big planet. Those stripes were storms, ferocious hurricanes that roared across the great world at hundreds of kilometers an hour. He shivered.

They drew closer to the tiny moon, pitted with craters, hardly larger than a medium-sized asteroid. In fact, that's what it was—a captured asteroid, dead and dull.

"I am not *just* a machine," the cow sniffed, offended. "I am a cyber-organic worker. I have many lifelike qualities. Cut me, will I not bleed?"

That was unfair. He had used the same argument on the aliens who had held him captive, and it hadn't influenced them either.

"Parts of me are made of meat, after all," the cow added. "Admittedly, humans did once eat meat."

Jack winced. That was an unpleasant thought. Certainly he would never cut a cow with a knife. The idea of actually *eating* one made him want to throw up.

"I'm not going to hurt you, Flossie," he said. "I only asked for a snack."

The cow just looked at him with its red glass eyes.

"Please?" he added.

"Certainly." Flossie rose from the carpet and reached underneath its own belly. A panel slid open, and a small glass of whiskey emerged. A moment later, two tasty burgers on a paper plate popped out as well. The cow handed the snack to its owner and sat down.

After a while, as Jack began munching and watching

the huge planet outside, the cow said, "*Thank you, Flossie.*"

"For Heck's sake—nag, nag, nag," Jack mumbled with his mouth full. "Oh, all right—thank you, dear cow. You're a very good machine."

Everyone knew the rule against interstellar cadets keeping pets or private robots in the Academy. The small seed Wilson—Tharam—had given him as a parting gift, with instructions to plant it in a bowl of milk, was strictly against regulations. Jack hid it inside his closet.

The seed grew and grew into a hairy ball, then started climbing out of the bowl of milk and wandering blindly around inside the closet, bumping its head on things. In less than a week, it grew as large as a dog, then larger still. Jack got the shock of his life when it started to talk to him. Then he realized that it was an artificial intelligence like the Mac. It asked him to provide scraps of steel and plastic and broken micronics, which Jack found in the recycling dumpster near the engine room, and then it ate them. In another week, it had grown to its full size as a cow. It could barely fit inside the closet any longer, but Jack made room for it by pushing more of his clothes under the bunk.

Jack shook his head, wiped the last of the burger juice from his chin. "Now, if you don't mind, Flossie, I'm going to watch—"

The planet's image on the screen vanished, replaced by the Academy's highest-ranking officer. Deputy Commandant Whimsel was wearing a peaked hat and

plenty of braid on her collar. She cleared her throat.

"Good afternoon, everybody. As you might have noticed, we are now orbiting the smallest of Bargleplod's five moons, Bink. This puts us approximately 100,000 kilometers from Bargleplod's surface. Bink's orbital speed is slightly faster than the rotation of the planet, so eventually we should see the whole world rotate underneath us. Cadets should take this opportunity to observe the planet's unusual meteorological patterns."

Commandant Whimsel's voice hardened. "Nobody—I repeat *nobody*, and that especially means you cadets—is to leave the Academy station and travel down to the surface of Bargleplod. It is a very dangerous place. An external elevator will carry a small party across to Bink, with the permission of the Bargleplod high command, to gather some rare minerals, and set up instruments to observe Bargleplod's storms. cLt. Jones will conduct a briefing in the usual quarters at 1600 hours. That is all."

"Dangerous," Jack scoffed. "Ha! A big fat planet, that's not dangerous. I know what 'dangerous' is. Why, Flossie, when I was—"

"Marooned on the planet with the Mac, yes, I have heard that story a few dozen times, Ensign."

Jack hated it when the cow cut him off like that. His fellow cadets had soon grown bored with hearing about his amazing adventure on the alien planet, and none of them believed anything he told them about his jaunt with Tharam to the future, if that's what had really happened, but it seemed very unfair that an organic

machine like Flossie could also give him a hard time about it. He sulked, and let his mind drift back to the relief he'd felt when he got back with Lt. Zamblott. And he was still proud of the way he'd rescued himself from the alien village to meet up with the rescue craft... He drifted off into a daydream.

"Jack! Jack!" Flossie interrupted him.

"What?" he growled.

"Jack! It is 1555. You must get to the briefing."

"Oh shit!" Jack jumped up and started poking around inside his closet for the cadet uniform jacket he had to wear to the briefing. "Have you seen my cap?"

"Under the bunk, near the bulkhead."

Jack found his cap and put it on, then took it off and brushed the red hairs off it. The hairs were from the cow, of course. Annoying thing, even if it did provide him with so many useful services. Not to mention tasty treats. His head buzzed a little. Maybe that shot of rye hadn't been such a good idea.

"Thanks, Flossie, cLt. Jones gets snaky if we're not on time. Now please be a good cow and stay hidden in the closet, you know I'm not meant to have you here with me in the Academy."

"Goodbye, Jack." The cow's voice was cut off as Jack slid the door shut behind him. The corridor was empty. Uh-oh, late again. He started running.

∞

Most of the time, the Academy was located beyond Mars and nearly to Jupiter, in a grand set of habitat

bubbles just a thousand kilometers from Wormhole One. Jack had spent two years as an interstellar cadet, getting his space-legs and learning how imperial Earth culture was uniting a league of species around the galaxy. From time to time, the Academy went exploring to give the cadets a taste of life beyond the habitat bubbles and the regular worlds.

Now he sat with a bunch of other cadets still in training, listening to Hortense Jones, who was ranting on about responsibility to all the inferior life forms of the galaxy as if she knew this first hand instead of just parroting notes provided by Commandant Whimsel. Jack yawned, trying to stay awake. This was such a waste of time! Just on the other side of the Academy's cloudy hull was a whole little moon named Bink, and far below that a gigantic world peopled by strange creatures. Why wasn't the cadet Lieutenant talking about them? This was supposed to be a briefing, not just another boring lecture.

To date, cLt. Jones reminded them all, nobody had ever found a civilization quite as technically advanced as Earth's, although a few like the warrior Xlaquat had space travel and powerful weapons. Persuasive negotiation had done the trick in every case. There hadn't been an interstellar war, she reminded them proudly, in more than two hundred years of space exploration, and no serious threat of one.

But that was before Bargleplod was discovered a few years earlier.

That made Jack sit up straight. He glanced around.

The other bored cadets were waking up as well, eyes bright, leaning forward in their chairs.

This new planet sounded as if it might be a whole lot of trouble. There were giant aliens down there, with big spaceships—and they didn't like Earth people.

Jack felt sure he was ready to handle trouble. Although he had turned twenty-one only three months ago, he had been a fully trained pod pilot for several years. Jack was proud of the way he'd acquitted himself in difficult situations. Yes, he knew how to handle trouble!

Abruptly, cLt. Jones started talking about the expedition to Bink.

"We will be taking two cadets across to the surface of the moonlet Bink," Jones told them. "We expect—"

"Aw!" cried one cadet, disappointed.

"Only two? One of them had better be a girl," shouted Julia Durango. She was due to graduate next month but was worried she didn't have enough missions under her belt.

"Calm down, you lot," cLt. Jones said. "As a matter of fact, one of the two *will* be a girl. cEnsigns Suzy Mugabe and John Wong have been selected—"

Jack felt a crushing sense of disappointment for an instant. John— Hey, wait a minute! That was *him!* Jack Wong! Envious faces swung around towards him, and a few friends came over to clap him on the back. Suzy was getting the same treatment.

Durango approached Jack's desk. "Good luck, Wong," she grunted, extending her hand. She leaned

forward and Jack drew back a little, sure she was going to say something spiteful. But all she whispered was: "Jack, meet me in corridor 15 after we get out. I have a deal for you."

She never called him "Jack," just shithead or Wong. He stiffened, preparing for headlong flight to safety.

"Ma'am?"

But she'd turned and was crossing the room to congratulate Suzy. CLt. Jones was shaking her head ruefully, waiting for the cadets to calm down. "Cadets dismissed!" she shouted. Everyone rushed out, eager to look at the big wall display in the Main Assembly room. Planet Bargleplod! Bink the moonlet!

Jack was jumping inside with excitement. He was going out to walk on the little moon. He vowed that this time he wouldn't do anything to mess up.

∞

Julia Durango pushed him up against the bulkhead. It hurt, and he yelped.

"Listen, you little shit," she said, gritting her teeth. "*I* deserve that trip out to the moonlet, not you. You've *already* been to a strange planet."

"I got *lost*," Jack yelped. She was already a large woman, and he was scared she'd sit on him. "Anyway, go and argue with cLt. Jones, it's not my idea."

"I know what *was* your idea," Durango said. She pulled away, so at least he couldn't smell her onion breath any more. "I know what you're hiding in your cabin."

What the hell? How could she have heard about Flossie? Jack felt nauseated. His best friend Rufus Rupert Trevor Dogge must have told her, even though Rufus was sworn to secrecy. No more burgers for *that* bastard. But wait, maybe Julia was just pretending to know something about his cow?

"Aw yeah?" He pushed himself away from the wall and straightened his uniform. "Who says I've got anything in my room?"

"Well, why have you been scrounging old micronics parts and things? Don't try to fool me, warthog. You've grown something in there, haven't you? What is it? A cyber-organic worker? A secret robot-animal translator?"

Corridor 15 was empty, but he could hear footsteps as people hurried up Corridor 14 to cheer and wave as the expedition set off. He had to hurry; if he was late maybe he'd miss the 'vator and get left behind. Durango would just love that.

"It's not a rat, okay. Anyway, so what if I'm doing some extra micronics work?"

But Julia Durango was smiling. She put her arm around him in a friendly way and picked a long red hair off his jacket sleeve.

"Listen, Jack, you never do extra work. This hair came off a cow. Your cow, Jack. Me and my friends, we'd really like to have a cow of our own. So how about you let us have yours. We can keep all this between ourselves." She gave him a sunny smile. "Hey, we'll even let you come over once a week and get a bottle or

two of hooch—for free!"

"What kind of deal's that?" Did she think he was stupid? "I like Flossie, she's my cow, not yours. I'm not letting you have her."

"Okay, I have another proposition for you," Durango told him. She reached inside her belt pouch, fumbled around and pulled out a handful of gleaming pellets, carefully guarding them from view with her other hand. "I get the cow, I don't blow the whistle on you, and you can have these."

Jack stared at them in fascination. They were beautiful: red as blood, green as grass, golden yellow, blue bright as the sky back at home. He had no idea what they were, but he wanted to touch them. He reached out, but Julia closed her fingers tightly.

"Not so quick, pea brain. First the cow."

"But what are they?"

"Don't you know anything? They're beans—biologically engineered assembler nanobes."

Jack went white. He knew what nanobes were, there'd been plenty of lessons about them. You couldn't see them with your eye. You couldn't even see them with a regular light microscope. Assembler nanobes were used to compile the synthetic food everyone ate on the Academy starship, but you had to get special permission to go anywhere near them. And the bio-engineered sort were the scariest. They had been constructed by experts out of broken-up microorganisms and pure code. And microorganisms could make you sick. Kill you, maybe.

"But they're *dangerous*! And *illegal*!"

"Don't be such a dweeb, Wong," Durango said. She started to put the beans back in her pouch. "These things can build anything your heart desires, but hey, if you're too chicken to—"

"No, no," Jack squealed. "I want them!"

Briefly he squeezed his eyes shut, imagined all the wonderful machines and tasty treats he could grow with a handful of beans. His eyes popped open again, filled with suspicion. "Yeah, right. If they're that good, why don't *you* use them? How come you want my poor cow when you can grow *anything*?"

The corridor was still empty. A distant siren was hooting.

"*Cadet John Wong*," the hidden speakers boomed up and down the corridor, "*please present yourself immediately at disembarkation port X-251.*"

Another moment's delay and the landing party would be going without him, for sure. He started to run along the corridor. Durango ran with him, clutching his arm.

"You idiot, beans need soil or rock to grow in. I thought they'd choose me to go to Bink so I could plant these, but no, they have to pick a little dweeb like you. So okay, if I can't use them, at least I can trade them. The cow for the beans. Deal?"

They reached the door to disembarkation port X-251. Jack passed his cabin key card to Durango. She took it with a smirk on her face, and handed him the gleaming pellets.

"If anything goes wrong, you don't know where

these came from, right?"

Jack was abruptly awash with doubts, but there was no time to back out now.

"Why should anything go wrong?" he asked.

"You're the one who got lost in space," Julia said. "You're the one who almost got eaten by aliens."

It was true. Jack shrugged and slipped through the door, snapping a quick and reluctant salute back at the cadet Lieutenant, which Durango did not return.

Minutes later, as he struggled into his spacesuit, he carefully pushed the beans into an outer pocket, then clomped off in his heavy boots towards the airlock.

∞

The expedition team straggled out in a line, bouncing lightly over the gray and brown moonlet. Several floaters loaded with equipment skimmed alongside. The Academy starship hung in the black sky behind them like another moon, with a long thin elevator reaching down to the surface like a blue plastic straw.

Once they got away from the Academy's elevator, the moonlet's own gravity took over. It was far weaker than inside the Academy, which generated an artificial inertial field. Jack felt as if he'd suddenly been inflated like a balloon. Every step he took threatened to throw him into that huge sky—and the looming face of the giant planet Bargleplod.

That planet was enormous, the biggest thing Jack had ever seen. Well no, that wasn't true. The Sun was much bigger, and so was Bargleplod's reddish sun,

which lit Bink with an odd glow. But you never got this close to suns. You'd be burned to a crisp. Bargleplod filled half the sky, rising up over the horizon like... like.... He couldn't think of anything else it reminded him of. You couldn't say it looked like a beach ball painted with hurricanes bigger than the planet Earth, that just sounded silly.

"No straggling, cadet Wong," said the lieutenant's voice in his ears.

"Sorry, ma'am," he sputtered, and bounced carefully along. Out here, his heavy boots felt as light as slippers. But they kept getting caught in cracks in the dusty rock, and he nearly fell on his face a couple of times.

"We could walk right around this silly little moonlet," Suzy said. "We could just keep going straight ahead and in a day or two we'd be back where we started."

That gave Jack a shock; he hadn't thought about it like that. It was true. Bink was a ball of rock, and he and the others were like ants crawling over it.

"We won't be going nearly that far, cadet Mugabe," a stern voice said on the radio—Dr. Fisherking, the Academy's chief scientist. Jack hadn't realized the doctor had joined the expedition, he seemed far too old. Why, the man must be sixty if he was a day, and as bald as a coot.

"An hour on the surface is all we've been allotted, and we have much to do. This moonlet is what we call a 'carbonaceous chondrite', very rich in carbon, clay-like hydrous silicate minerals and other valuable

elements for the Academy's construction nanobes."

Jack rolled his eyes at Suzy through his helmet visor. His cow had tried to explain that carbon-ayshus-whatever, but it had skidded right off the top of his brain.

"As well," Dr. Fisherking was saying, "Bink is perfectly positioned to observe Bargleplod from a safe distance. When we reach that cliff ahead, we will deploy our instruments. No slacking, I say. I want everyone to pull his weight."

Jack couldn't help laughing. "Not much weight here to pull."

"Who said that?"

Uh-oh. Jack kept his head down and his mouth shut. After a moment, Dr. Fisherking said, "Well, never mind that. I want no horsing around, and less backchat."

∞

At the cliff, everyone collected their assigned floaters and set to work. Jack's carried an X-ray telescope to place 300 meters off to the west, while Suzy headed east with a radio telescope. All this could have been done by robots, AIs and cows, of course, but the Academy liked to keep its human crew trained for emergencies and on its toes.

To his amazement, Jack found that in just a few minutes he was out of sight of the others. Bink was tiny, and its horizon was only...how far off?

"Calculator," Jack said to his suit's artificial intelligence system. It was just as humorless as his lost Mac, but it could do mathematics with blazing speed. "How

far is it to the horizon on Bink?"

In a drab voice, his system told him: "Bink is a little over 32 kilometers in diameter. Using the formula d equals h plus r squared minus—"

"Forget the formula," Jack said. "Just tell me."

"Roughly 220 meters," the machine said. Was that a surly note in its voice? Jack rather hoped so. "Of course I could give you a highly accurate figure to sixteen decimal places if you wish. My pleasure, really, sir."

"No, thank you."

A piercing whistle sounded in his right ear. "By the way, you should stop now. This is the place for the X-ray telescope to be mounted."

"All right, all right, keep your shirt on."

"I am a machine, I do not wear a—"

Jack tuned the stupid thing out, took his equipment off the floater and set it on an expanse of brown rock. The six thin legs of the telescope felt about carefully, then squatted. Puffs of dust rose, and instantly fell again, since there was no air to hold the dust up. The X-ray telescope had drilled its feet into the rock. The snout of the thing swiveled, hunting for its target. Jack followed its angle, and found himself staring the planet Bargleplod full in the face.

It hung directly in front of him like a painted wall, blocking out most of the sky. Jack shivered, glancing over his shoulder for the rest of the team. Nobody in sight. He took an eager step closer to the floater, just for the company, and nearly flew up into the sky. That was how weak the gravity was on Bink. Shuddering,

he clutched the floater. It's all right, he told himself. True, they can't see me and I can't see them, but the communicator still works.

He blinked. Nobody could see him, that was absolutely true.

So this was an ideal chance to plant his beans.

Jack felt in his outer pocket with his gloved fingers. There they were, beautiful, gleaming pellets. He held them in his open palm, seeing their bright colors against the white glove. No, this was foolish. He'd get caught. Anyway, even if he planted them he'd never get another chance to come out on the surface of Bink and collect whatever treasures these beans manufactured from the bare rock of the moonlet.

Wait a minute—

D'oh! *That* was Julia Durango's intention!

He couldn't believe he'd been so stupid. Obviously she and her friends would arrange to come out on the *next* expedition, and they'd find the bean machine fully grown, and harvest all its goodies.

Jack would get nothing for his pains!

He groaned again as another cruel thought struck him. He'd lost his faithful cow Flossie, and for no gain. In his foolish greed for these worthless beans, he'd given Julia his cabin key card. While he was out here wallowing around in micro-gravity, she and her nasty friends would have kidnapped his dear cow and taken it to her own cabin. They were probably gorging themselves and drinking synthesized aged whiskey right now!

"I'll take these stupid beans back," he muttered. "I'll give them back and tell her she's got to return poor Flossie at once."

"I beg your pardon?" said his suit's system. "Are you addressing me? My name is certainly not Flossie."

"Oh, go to sleep," Jack said. He closed his hand and shoved it back inside his pocket.

Something tumbled, dancing in the red-brown light of Bargleplod's sun.

"Oh shit!"

One of the beans had fallen out of his padded glove. It shone blood-red. In slow motion, it tumbled towards the rock.

Jack lurched forward, grabbed at it. His outstretched fingers touched the bean, but that just made things worse. It flew away, bounced on the rocky surface, rolled towards a shadowed crack in the gray stone. It kept rolling, about to vanish forever.

"No, no, come back," Jack bleated. Stepping forward several steps, his boot crushed the bean into fine powder.

"Alert! Alert!" cried his on-board system. "I detect an unauthorized release of bio-engineered nanobes!"

"Pipe down!" Jack rasped. He was so angry with himself he wanted to bite his hand, but his glove was in the way. "How can I get the nanobes back?"

"You cannot," his suit said. "They are only the size of microbes. Now that the bean's outer casing is broken, they have been released. I am going to have to alert Dr. Fisherking immediately."

"Oh please don't do that," Jack cried. "Let me try to scrape them up."

"It is my duty. I cannot delay."

Really it was Jack's duty to report the accident, of course, and he knew it. He pulled himself together, gasping for air in his fright and shame. What a fool! What a clumsy oaf! They'd throw him out of the Academy for this. He'd have to go back to Earth and see the burning shame in his parents' eyes. A failed cadet, denied the franchise. It was too horrible to think about, so he decided to think about it later. For now, he had his duty.

"You're quite right," he told his system. "This could be an emergency. Please notify the Academy immed—"

But he couldn't hear his own words. Something was happening under his feet, and the shock of it went up through his legs and shook his spacesuit like a giant rattle. There was no air to carry the sound waves to his ears, but the vibrations slamming though his suit created a terrible din. He started to scream, and heard that.

He was flung away from the floater. For a long moment he hung suspended in black space, and then the surface came boiling up to meet him.

The ground was alive. Something terrible was happening to the placid, ancient rock of the moonlet. Something awful was crawling out of the stone, twisting and searching like a blind worm or a snake.

It reached upward and wrapped itself around his leg.

Jack shrieked.

"Cease struggling, Jack," his suit told him. "We are in the grip of a bucky fiber tentacle."

"A *what*?" For a moment, he nearly lost control of his bladder, something you're always seriously advised not to do inside a short-time minimal spacesuit.

"The nanobes are digesting materials from the surface of Bink and growing some sort of tentacle. It has you in its grip."

"A *tentacle*?" Jack screamed in horrified disbelief, and the loud sound of it rang inside his helmet, half deafening him. He shook his head, bewildered. "Why would a bean make a tentacle?"

"You really must calm down, cadet Wong," his suit said calmly, "bucky fibers have sharp edges, there is a risk that they might damage your suit and cause your air to leak away into space. If they entered your helmet, they could put your eye out."

Jack squeezed his eyes tight shut and didn't move a muscle for many seconds. Something was pushing him, faster and faster. He started shouting at the top of his voice.

"Lt. Jones!" He switched channels frantically. "Dr. Fisherking!" Nobody replied.

The horrid thing, whatever it was, had thrown him into space, and then cut off his radio link to the rest of his squad! They couldn't hear him, and he couldn't hear them. "Calling the Academy! Cadet Rufus Dogge! Help me! Please help me! *Flossie*!"

Nothing, just the hiss of interstellar radio noise from

a billion mindless stars.

"I'm sorry to report that your radio antennae have been severed. We have lost radio contact with the expedition crew and Academy ship."

"Well, *do* something about it! Can't you fix it?"

"I am activating repair procedures. Please wait."

"Hurry up, please." Jack cleared his visor and stared out.

Bargleplod was directly overhead. The bucky fiber tentacle would push him into its thick atmosphere and he'd burn up like a blazing meteor.

No, he told himself. Don't be ridiculous. You won't be going fast enough to combust. Anyway, Commandant Whimsel won't let that happen. She'll send a rescue pod after me.

He relaxed a fraction and opened his eyes.

Bargleplod hung over him like a vast wall that he was about to smash into.

He shut his eyes again, and started shaking.

"Please, cadet Wong, you must remain calm. You are being held and propelled by pure bucky fibers. They could cut your spacesuit to ribbons."

"Stop saying that," Jack ordered in a rasping voice.

The suit fell silent. Jack toggled his visor to multi-display mode, and looked around through the small camera buds mounted on various parts of his suit. As he flicked from one screen image to the next, he started to grasp exactly what was happening to him—and the danger he was in.

It was as strange as some childhood fairytale come

to life. But this time it was real.

It was the biologically engineered assembler nanobes.

They were building something—no, they were *growing* something, just like a seed had grown his cow Flossie out of a bowl of milk and old spare parts.

The pictures from the cameras on his back and right boot showed something so strange it seemed to freeze his blood in his veins.

A kind of thick shining thread was wrapped around one leg and his waist. From there, it stretched back all the way to the receding curve of Bink's surface. Black leaves thrust out along its length, catching and swallowing the light of Bargleplod's red sun. Solar panels, Jack realized. The thing was powering itself with solar energy.

And it continued to grow, like toothpaste squeezed from an endless tube.

As he watched, the moonlet fell away beneath him. He was stuck to the end of something like an enormous out-of-control stalk. It wasn't a tentacle around his waist – it was a tendril. He laughed grimly. He'd dropped a bean, and it was growing a beanstalk. So much for his idea of growing whatever he wanted.

The beanstalk snaked out further and further into space, bearing him with it. Tiny figures below waved their arms, looking like frightened insects. He was carried higher as he watched, faster and faster, and suddenly he couldn't see them any longer. The moonlet dwindled into the distance. The gleaming stalk and its

thirsty black leaves grew and grew, pushing outward, throwing off brilliant beams of reddish light from its brand-new bucky fiber coils.

"How far can it grow?" Jack wailed.

"As far as the beans want," his suit responded. "Bucky fiber is a precise arrangement of carbon atoms, which are plentiful in Bink's crust. The nanobes are digging into the moonlet. As long as they have enough carbon they can produce bucky fiber."

"Is it going to break?" Jack imagined himself spinning off into space.

"Cadet Wong, remember your lessons! Bucky fiber is an extremely strong structure built of sixty carbon atoms. Carbon is an essential element of all living things, and bucky fibers have some characteristics of living cells. The beans will ensure that the bucky fiber is strong enough for their purposes."

But Jack was still terrified. What scared him was the size of the thing the nanobes were building. He was stuck on it like a worm on a fishing line.

"It's a skyhook, isn't it," he whispered.

A skyhook was a cable that stretched all the way from an orbiting satellite to a planet's surface. Skyhooks were made of incredibly strong bucky fiber. Just like this horrible thing.

"It certainly looks like a skyhook," his suit said. "I believe your bean is trying to bridge the gap between the moonlet Bink and the planet Bargleplod."

For a moment, Jack's head spun so badly he thought he was about to faint. He pulled himself together, as if

he were climbing hand over hand up a cliff. "You mean I'm going to be—" He couldn't finish.

"If this goes on," his suit said, "you will be carried all the way to the surface of the planet Bargleplod on the end of the skyhook."

He shuddered. What if the tendril lost its grip on him and he fell off? No, surely he would be dead of starvation and suffocation before the skyhook reached Bargleplod's dangerous surface.

"I'm doomed," he moaned. "I'm totally screwed."

In every direction except straight ahead, or up, or whatever it was, space was very dark. Jack couldn't see the stars unless he turned off most of the displays in his helmet, because his eyes adjusted to the light, and starlight is very faint even in deep space. Worse still, every time he glanced up, he was dazzled by the vast, shifting red-orange-yellow-brown of the giant planet's storms.

Bargleplod shone by the reflected light of its own sun, of course. It wasn't like a neon light, glowing from its own energy. Like the Earth and the Moon, it caught the light of its sun and flung it back out again. That was enough, though, to turn it into something like a vivid painting illuminated by a reddish spotlight. When Jack looked directly at Bargleplod, his eyes started to water.

"Cadet Wong, are you crying?"

"Certainly not," Jack sniffled. He couldn't wipe his eyes, because his hands were on the outside of the face panel and he couldn't open that without letting all his air out. He blinked the tears away. "It's just the bright

light, it hurts my eyes."

"This might help," his suit said. It polarized the helmet's visor, cutting off some of the dazzle. Like sun visors at the beach. The thought of the warm beach with its honey-colored sand made him choke up. He might never dig his toes down into the sand again, or go swimming in the sea with his family and friends! He would die out here in the cold loneliness of space and never see his—

"—det Wong," a voice said in his ears. "Are you receiving this message?"

"Yes! Yes!" Jack shouted. That was Commandant Whimsel's voice on the open channel. A surge of relief ran through his body. "Can you hear me, Ma'am? This thing tore my antennae right off!" The suit must have managed to rebuild them in the meantime.

"We have you in sight, cadet Wong. You appear to be trapped on the growing end of a bucky fiber skyhook."

Jack shook with relief. He was saved! He twisted his head around, looking for the rescue pod.

No pod. Just blackness, and, right ahead, the vast open mouth of the planet Bargleplod.

"Where are you?" he shouted anxiously. "I can't see you."

"Cadet Wong, we have a small problem."

Oh, great. *They* had a problem. Didn't they know *his* problem was far worse than any problem *they* might have? No, wait a minute, she must mean they had a problem with his *rescue.*

Jack felt cold again, cold and frightened.

"What problem, Ma'am?"

"You appear to have stolen a skyhook bean. Once activated, the bean follows a set program unless it's over-ridden by its authorization code."

"*Stolen*?" That was so unfair. "I didn't steal it, I swapped it. I swapped it for my cow with cadet—" Just in time, he shut his mouth. You didn't rat on your fellow cadets. Loyalty to your crew mates, one for all and all for one. Even if they were spoiled and nasty bullies, like Julia Durango, you still didn't rat on them.

"You had a cow on board the Academy?" She sounded outraged.

"Begging the Commandant's pardon, ma'am," said cLt. Jones on the open line, "I believe I can handle this matter with my squad." It seemed to Jack that there was a tight edge to her tone.

"Certainly, Jones. In due course."

In the background, Jack heard Lt. Zamblott's laugh booming out, "A cow? He had an unauthorized *cow* in his cabin? Good Lord, I did the very same thing on my first—" The voice broke off abruptly.

"We'll deal with your breach of that rule at a later time, cadet Wong. Right now we have a more serious problem."

Jack shivered again, hearing her hard tone. His suit was being shaken as the skyhook grew and grew, plunging him ever closer to the raging atmosphere of the planet Bargleplod. If they didn't pull him off the thing soon, he'd plunge into the swirling clouds of the alien world.

The strange thing was, he suddenly realized, the planet didn't seem to be getting any closer. He put that thought aside, because Commandant Whimsel was speaking again, in a voice that was obviously meant to soothe him. Yeah, right. It was as soothing as the growl of a Doberman.

"The bean that grew this skyhook is programmed for self-defense. Do you see those solar panels it's building all along the length of the cable?"

"Yes ma'am." It would be hard to miss them. Now that they were stretched out so far, overlapping each other to catch as much sunlight as possible, they completely blocked his view of the moonlet Bink.

"They are powering a laser array that will shoot down and destroy any meteor or other foreign body approaching the cable from space."

"Any foreign—? But Commandant Whimsel, you're not foreign and inferior, you're a *human*!"

"Listen to me, son. The cable's simple artificial intelligence assumes that any unauthorized body approaching it from space is dangerous," the Commandant explained patiently, or at least as patiently as you could imagine a Doberman ever getting. "Jack, I don't suppose you have the authorization code, do you?"

In a very small voice, he said, "No, ma'am. Sorry."

"That's a considerable nuisance," the Commandant sighed, "A skyhook cable is designed to stretch between a satellite and the surface of whatever world it orbits. That is a very long way indeed. It cannot afford to be pierced by a meteor from space, or by a satellite in the

same orbit running into it, or suffer a deliberate attack by an enemy. Even a minor collision might snap it."

"Oh." Jack imagined what would happen to a skyhook hundreds of thousands of kilometers long if something broke it in half. The lower half, freed, would collapse towards the ground, faster and faster, thousands of tons of bucky fiber cable slamming into the atmosphere. Some would burn like a falling meteor, the rest would smash into the planet like a huge whip. Maybe it would pulverize whole continents.

"It has to defend itself, do you see, Jack?"

He shuddered. The skyhook was building laser cannons, that's what the Commandant meant. It was making powerful weapons to defend itself from anything coming towards it. It was powering up to blast any intruder. And that included a rescue pod.

He was stuck here for good. The tip of the skyhook would push him into Bargleplod's swirling storms. And there was no way anyone could get here to save him.

With the greatest effort, he forced himself not to burst into tears. Gritting his teeth together, he said, "Aye, aye, ma'am. I understand."

"I'm glad you do, Jack," Commandant Whimsel told him, and closed the transmission.

∞

"I have information that you require, cadet Wong," said Jack's suit.

"What is it now?"

"I have calculated our orbit, and the growing tip of the skyhook is moving faster than the surface of the planet. Look at your helmet display as I run this educational applet."

The visor went opaque, and an image started running in the left-hand corner, with a bunch of equations and calculations showing in the right-hand side. Orbital ballistics, not really Jack's favorite subject. It was the sort of thing he far preferred to leave to his suit AI. His old AI, the Mac, had nagged him constantly to do this kind of homework when he was stranded on the alien world. That planet had seemed horrible at the time, but now he wished he was back there, sitting beside the aliens at their stinking fire, watching them eat disgusting things full of wriggling maggots. For that matter, he wished he'd stayed with the Rear Admiral in the future, if that's where it was, in the Great Flapping Cat Café.

That would be far better than falling to his death.

He dragged his gibbering mind back to the images on his display. They showed Bink circling around Bargleplod, which was spinning, as planets tend to do. The speed of the moon was a little faster than the spin of the planet.

Uh-oh.

"Bargleplod's day is only a bit over eight hours long," the suit continued, "but Bink goes around the planet every seven hours."

"So Bink is moving at 64,000 kilometers an hour," Jack said with a sinking heart, reading the data in his

displays. "But Bargleplod is only rotating at 56,000 kilometers an hour." It was incredibly fast, thirty-three times faster than the Earth's own spin, but not as fast as Bink's orbiting speed. Then he saw what his suit meant. "Oh my god."

"Indeed," the AI said despondently. "The vector sum of three tangential velocities is going to drag us both to our doom."

It was as plain as the nose on his face, which was due to be torn off his face when he and the tip of the ever-growing skyhook hit the planet's surface at 8,000 kilometers an hour. More than two klicks a second.

Jack watched the animation on the display. It showed how a standard skyhook needed to be grown from geostationary orbit, with the satellite, or asteroid or moon, circling the planet at exactly the same speed as the planet rotated, so it always remained fixed above the same point on the surface beneath it as it lengthened. The reason it got longer, of course, was because a bean seed was gobbling up raw material and converting it into pure buckminsterfullerene for the cable.

At the same time, another seeded cable was stretching away in the opposite direction, rising straight up away from the primary world. That one exactly balanced the skyhook dropping to the surface.

With a shock, Jack realized that on the distant far side of the moonlet Bink, another cable must already be rising. The skyhook seeds in the bean must have tunneled straight through the middle of the moon, raising the distant twin of the cable that now held him

trapped him in its grasp.

But that was of no concern to him. He moaned in despair.

"It's going to drag me along the ground, right? Like hitting the ground in a pod at hypersonic speeds?"

"Well, the cable will be slowed down by the atmosphere," the suit responded. "It will certainly be whipping violently. This suit will act like a kite in a strong wind." It paused. "Actually, it is more likely you will cook to death from aerodynamic heating when that point is reached." The suit's voice had gone beyond despondency into frank horror.

"I've got to get off," Jack whispered, his throat dry as sandpaper.

His eyes remained riveted to the screen display.

"No, wait," the suit said. "Unlike me, you are a frail organism with tiresome needs."

It was true. The numbers showed it plainly. As he had suspected, long before the growing skyhook hit the planet's thick atmosphere, he would starve to death, or his air would run out.

This bucky fiber cable he was stuck to was growing at a ferocious rate, almost impossible to grasp. The nanobes were chewing up the rock of Bink in appalling quantities, spinning the carbon into cable, extruding the cable into space at fifty kilometers an hour. It was an insane roller coaster ride into the heavens.

But still it was too slow.

The figures did not lie. The cable would not reach the rushing surface of Bargleplod for nearly 2,000 hours.

Three months, in other words. Give or take.

He didn't have food or water or air in this spacesuit for more than three days.

He was one doomed space cadet.

∞

"Cadet Wong, you must slow your heart-rate and breathing. Perhaps some more orbital ballistics review would be appropriate at this time."

A set of multi-choice questions appeared on his helmet screen.

"What?" Jack was outraged. "You can't expect me to do *homework* when I'm stuck on the end of a skyhook."

"There is a slim chance that you might be rescued," the AI told him.

"This is so unfair," Jack muttered, but he set to work answering the quiz. After a while he realized that it was a good distraction. He was almost irritated when the suit interrupted him.

"There is an unusual disturbance in the planet's atmosphere."

"Where?" Jack swiveled his head, looked up. The skyhook cable had him gripped tightly by his leg and waist, and Bargleplod loomed directly overhead. He couldn't see anything, just the great silent storms rushing across the huge world.

"A cloaked Bargleplod vessel is rising into space. I believe it intends to attack the skyhook cable. I will attempt to communicate with its crew."

Out of nowhere, rushing towards him was an enor-

mous— What? It looked like a castle standing on a hill, surrounded by rivers and purple fields with some sort of animals grazing, and clouds overhead. It seemed more like a piece of countryside hurtling through space than any spacecraft he'd ever seen.

"We are receiving a transmission from the Bargleplod vessel."

His visor's screen jiggled, and he was looking at several aliens. Bargleplods! His stomach squirmed in terror. They were said to dislike humans. They were gigantic. Their teeth were very large and square, far more frightening than Wilson's. Tharam's. The one at the front barked something in a terrifying voice.

"I have not yet downloaded Bargleplodian," the suit said. "I will do so now."

"Well, hurry up," Jack muttered. The Bargleplods didn't look as though they should be kept waiting.

The Bargleplod barked again, grinding its teeth.

Jack's suit suddenly spoke in the same booming, dreadful tones as the aliens. Jack jumped, banging the top of his head on his helmet.

"What did you say?" Jack asked.

"I just told it that its dog eats kitty litter."

"*What?* Don't upset it." But it was too late. The Bargleplod was leaping about in a fury, throwing things, tearing out tufts of fur from its huge ears. "What's it saying now?"

"Hmm." The suit was silent for a moment. "Let me see if I can translate it. It went something like this: Fee, fi, fo, fum, I smell the blood of a human man!"

"Aargh!" Jack shrieked. "How can it smell my blood?"

"I think it's just trying to scare you."

"Well, it's working." But the jeering Bargleplod had been pushed aside by an even larger specimen, which was roaring and beating its chest.

"Oh," the suit said. "I don't think you would wish to hear a translation of *that*."

Jack's teeth were chattering with fear, but he said bravely, "Go on, tell me."

"Very well. I think it said: Let him be alive or let him be dead, I'll grind his bones to make my bread."

A bright light erupted in front of his visor. Blinking dazzled eyes, Jack asked, "Did the skyhook fire on the aliens?"

"Yes. The laser cannon array that protects the skyhook from damage has been triggered by the proximity of the Bargleplod spacecraft. The Bargleplod craft appears to be unharmed. It must be protected by powerful shielding."

"Oh great," Jack said.

"At least you won't starve and suffocate inside me, or be dragged along the surface of the planet at 8,000 kilometers an hour," the suit said in an encouraging voice.

"Well, that's a great relief," Jack shouted. "That's a real comfort. No, I'll just have my bones ground up into Bargleplodian *bread*!"

He dimmed his visor's display, so he could see what was going on. Explosions of light showed that the

skyhook was still trying to shoot the ridiculous craft out of the sky, without success.

The Bargleplod castle, with its rivers and purple fields, was rising towards him like a huge decorated cake. The ship seemed to be slowing down, but it was unharmed by the energy bolts.

He was condemned to end his days as the meat and bread in a Jack-sandwich.

∞

Commandant Whimsel came back on the channel. "Cadet Wong, we have established contact with the Bargleplod cruiser *Snardly Bink*." She sounded cross. "What have you been saying to the Bargleplod captain?"

"Um, I said I liked his dog," Jack said weakly. It wasn't really a lie. For all he knew, Bargleplod dogs *did* eat kitty litter, and anyway it was the suit that said it.

"A weird thing to say to an alien captain," the Commandant said. "We're trying to rescue you before the *Snardly Bink* reaches your end of the skyhook. If by any chance they get to you first—"

"He said he'd grind my bones for bread!" Jack yelped.

"I'm sure the captain meant nothing of the sort." The Commandant didn't sound too convinced, though. "But just in case he did, we've sent help. Look down the skyhook cable. They should arrive at any moment."

Something grabbed Jack's foot.

He screamed in fright.

"Hey, calm down, fish breath!"

"Julia Durango?" She was the last person he'd expected to see out here.

"Hey, nerd man!" said another familiar voice. Someone in a spacesuit swung forward at the end of a spacewalk tether. The helmet came close, hanging upside down. A face looked in at him.

"Rufus?" Jack felt a burst of happiness. His pal! "You old Dogge! And *Flossie*? But how did you get here without being fried by the skyhook's lasers?"

"There is no time to chatter, Jack Wong," the cow replied. "I rushed them to your rescue."

As the two cadets prised the bucky fiber tendril from around Jack's legs and waist, freeing him from the skyhook, they attached a spacewalk tether in its place. Jack floated around and found himself gazing into the red glass eyes of his cyber-organic worker.

"I am glad to see that you are well," the cow said. "Now, if you will join your companions on my back, we should return to what remains of the moonlet Bink."

Rufus and Julia tugged him lightly towards the cow. The machine was now twice as long as it had been that morning. It would never fit into his closet now. They must have been force-feeding it. Just as well, because there was barely room for all three of them in their bulky suits.

Flossie's legs extended ahead and behind like long sliding tubes of darkness, and the feet grasped the gleaming bucky fiber cable with finger-like toes of

steel. The cow started to run back down the cable, dodging the outflung black solar cells, ducking in and out of their great shadows.

"Why doesn't the skyhook attack us?" Jack asked.

"Because we're already *on* it," Rufus explained in a rather irritating, condescending tone.

"What did you expect," Julia added. Her tone was even more contemptuous. "Skyhooks are elevators, after all. They're meant to link the ground with the sky, so people can ride up and down them in comfort. You don't want your elevator to start shooting at you!"

Jack fell silent, clinging to the cow's back. The machine was still speeding up. The helmet display showed that they were moving along the cable at well over 100 klicks an hour, more than twice as fast as the cable was growing outward from Bink. "Wait a minute," he said. "How can you run an elevator up and down a cable with all these huge solar panels sticking out of it?"

"Don't you know *anything?*" Durango asked, jabbing him with her elbow. "They shed their solar cells when they're fully grown. Like trees lose their leaves."

"But that's only in winter." Jack was confused.

"Actually they don't *shed* them," Rufus said. "They *absorb* them."

He felt he wasn't quite keeping up with this conversation. Something was nagging at his mind. Something was trying to get his attention. Some urgent thought was trying—

"Aargh!" he shrieked. "We've forgotten about the

Bargleplods!" Where had the alien gone?

The *Snardly Bink* reappeared, laser blasts bouncing from its defense shields. It was huge. Jack huddled into the red hairy back of his cow as the spacecraft drew closer.

The giant Bargleplod captain came out onto the roof of the castle and shook one vast fist at the humans and their galloping cow before veering away out of laser range.

"It's saying Fee, Fi, Fo, Fum again," Jack's suit said helpfully. "Should I reply?"

∞

"Now hear this, cadets." Commandant Whimsel voice was crisp and stern in their helmet speakers. "We have been discussing the situation with the Bargleplod high command. They believe it's your fault that their moonlet Bink is being eaten."

"*Our* fault?" yelped Jack. "How can it be *our*— Oh."

It *was* his fault, he realized. If he hadn't taken the beans outside to plant on the surface of the moonlet, none of this would have happened. True, he'd changed his mind and decided not to plant them, but then he'd clumsily dropped one. He felt in his pocket. Yes, at least the remaining beans were safe. He vowed to hand them over to the Commandant the moment he got back to the Academy. She'd know how to dispose of the dangerous things. He couldn't begin to imagine how Durango had got hold of them in the first place.

"The Bargleplods want us to stop the cable from

growing any further. They say they did not give us permission to build a skyhook elevator, and that it's an invasion of their space. And so it is."

"You mean they're not going to eat me if we can deactivate the nanobes?" Jack sagged with relief. "He said he'd grind my bones."

"Eat you? Whatever do you mean?" The Commandant sounded baffled. Someone muttered in the background. "Oh, I see. Cadet Wong, your suit has miss-translated. The Bargleplod captain is wishing you well, and hopes that your bones will be returned to the ground." She paused. "You know, not get left out there in space." That didn't sound any better. "Oh, never mind that now. The point is, we need to get hold of the authorization code to switch off the compiler bean. We have to stop this now."

"I have more beans in my pocket," he said. "Would they have the same authorization code?" Jack pulled out the remaining beans. They gleamed in the darkness of space, caught in the shafts of light of Bargleplod's sun as the cow passed between the shadows of the solar cells.

A blazing bolt from the skyhook lasers jolted the Bargleplod craft. It swung slightly, struck the cable. A deep, awful gonging went through the legs of the racing cow and up into Jack's spacesuit and body. His hand opened as he grabbed for the cow's neck. The beans floated away.

"Oh no," he shouted in horror. "Someone catch them before they float away into space—"

But there was no time for anyone to do anything. It was up to Jack himself. He grabbed Rufus by one glove and flung himself away into space, his other hand outstretched. Most of the beans had already spun out of reach, but one was moving more slowly. With a jerk that almost wrenched his elbow out of its socket, he closed his fist over it.

"Gotcha!"

Julia and Rufus pulled him back to the cow. He stayed there for a long moment, shuddering, then called the waiting Academy.

"What should I do with the bean?"

"Give it to your cow," Commandant Whimsel said in a very calm voice. "Just place the bean in its mouth to decode it. Your cow will transmit the authorization code and shut-down message to us."

Doubtfully, Jack held out his hand towards the cow's head. He kept his fingers tightly closed. Without turning, the cow sent a long, long pink tongue lolloping over its shoulder and nuzzled at his glove. Jack forced himself to relax his grip. Flossie's tongue wrapped itself around the bean, and vanished back inside the cow's head. There was a blast of radio noise: the code being transmitted to the Academy.

Flossie gulped and burped loudly. They all heard it through their helmet speakers. Jack stared at Rufus. Rufus stared back at Jack. They both stared at Julia Durango, and she stared at them. Flossie turned her head over her shoulder and winked at them. They started laughing helplessly, clinging to the cow's artifi-

cial fur, punching each other weakly.

Through Flossie's racing mechanical feet, they felt another jolt.

"The skyhook has ceased growing," the cow reported in a pleased tone. "Shortly, it will begin to resorb the cable and rebuild the surface of the moonlet Bink."

This news seemed to satisfy the Bargleplod captain. As Jack watched, the great space-castle *Snardly Bink* swung about like a purple dream and drifted away into black space.

The Bargleplod captain sent a final transmission, appearing briefly on Jack's helmet display. He roared terribly.

"He bids you farewell, loathsome young human," his suit translated. "He wishes never to see you again, but hopes that your bones remain inside your flesh for many years, where nobody need look at them."

Jack shook his head. "Tell him I feel exactly the same way."

All of a sudden, he was terribly hungry. He needed a giant burger with the lot, and a shot of whiskey. His eyes started to water again, and his throat compressed. No, he didn't. What he wanted was some chocolate chip cookies and a long glass of cold milk.

"Hurry up, Flossie," he told his cow, wrapping his arms tightly about its neck.

They raced through the darkness and the light, and the cloudy glass globe of the Academy hung welcomingly ahead of them in the interstellar night.

CHAPTER FOUR
TIME

Newly-minted Ensign John Wong returned his dress uniform to the closet. A stray red hair floated in the cycled air and attached itself lightly to one sleeve of his space-black garb with its silver piping. He brushed it free, and a sentimental tear ran down his cheek.

"I wish you'd been there for the ceremony, Flossie," he muttered.

But his cow had been conscripted to serve as the Academy's new mascot.

At least Gillian had been able to make it to the ceremony. Ensign Durango whistled when she saw her. "What are you doing with such a good-looking girlfriend, Wong? And how come we never heard of her before?"

"Gillian's my sister, you asshole," Jack muttered back. "And she doesn't play for your team, so forget it."

That earned him a sharp jab in the ribs, but it was worth it. He was sick and tired of Julie Durango's gibes. Probably she was still in a snit about losing the cow she'd hornswoggled from Jack in exchange for the nanobeans that almost caused an interstellar inci-

dent, or maybe a war. That should have earned them both a spell in the brig, or worse—expulsion from the Academy. Somehow, though (perhaps through the mysterious intervention of Rear Admiral Ricardo Fortesque Martinique, ret.), they were let off with a withering warning from Commandant Whimsel and allowed to graduate with the rest of their Company.

∞

"You already know the planet," said the officer from the Diplomatic Corps, "you know the indigenous people—"

"People!" Jack was outraged. "They stink, they eat maggots."

"Those are the very qualities you should see as a challenge. We could hardly send you off to bring Earth Values to folk who already use *eau-de-cologne* and eat hamburgers. You'll be in your element, Wong. You and your mission team."

"Who else is going, sir?"

"A civilian anthropologist. You already know her. Name of Wong."

"Gillian? My sister?"

"So I'm told. And Ensign Durango will be an invaluable member."

"Oh no."

"Oh yes."

His heart sank. "She'll be in command, then."

"No, oddly enough. Someone upstairs thinks your previous experience with the Grawnks qualifies you

for leadership this time."

"Thank you, sir!" Jack's breast swelled with pride, an unaccustomed sensation.

"Good god, don't thank *me*. Hardly my idea."

"Oh. Who else is in the team, sir?"

"Alien chap by the name of Fang aka Wilson aka Tharam."

"Wilson! He's not even human."

"Equal Opportunity should be your watchword, Wong. Eq Op as it's called in the Corps."

Jack looked the officer in the eye, then blinked from the strain of meeting that unyielding gaze and lowered his own eyes. "May I ask a question, sir?"

"Permission to ask a question granted. Can't guarantee an answer."

"Did Rear Admiral Martinique have a hand in selecting this team?"

"Classified info, Wong. But since you ask, affirmative."

"That figures," he muttered.

"It does, indeed. Here's one thing you should know, Ensign. There's been a bit of uncertainty about the temporal coordinates. You might have to put your chronometers forward a bit. Or back a bit."

"One usually does, sir."

"Only the hours and minutes, usually. This time it might involve the year. Or the century."

"Time travel, sir? I thought that was impossible."

"Possible, Wong, possible. That final wormhole you stumbled into is an unreliable bastard, timewise."

∞

Three wormhole transits later, Ensign Wong brought his pod to a soft landing in the same clearing where he had crash-landed as a callow nineteen year old cadet. "Now remember," he said to his crew, "it's our Macs that they are going to treat as gods, not us."

"Yes, Ensign Wong. I think we've all got that item of information mastered," Ensign Durango said, curling her lip one millimeter short of insubordination. Clearly she was still riled that Jack was in charge of the mission.

"Here they come, now," Jack said.

The crew looked at the screen displaying the immediate outside world, flickering with analyses of temperature, atmospheric composition, humidity, noise levels, possible toxins, and a hundred other parameters. All still seemed safely within human tolerance levels, although still as uncomfortably hot as it had been during his previous visit. On the edge of the clearing, half a dozen aliens stood looking towards the pod.

"You didn't tell us they wore clothes," Gillian Wong said. "Hell, Jack, you could have been a bit more informative."

"They didn't. They didn't wear clothes."

"Well, they do now. Just look at those threads. They must have plaited them out of dried grass."

"Maybe it's a different season. But it's certainly not winter," Jack said.

"Maybe," Durango said, "someone has been teaching them to wear clothes."

"Who?" Gillian said. "This planet is off-limits. No

one else has visited this place. At least, not as far as we know."

"How much do we know? Maybe we'll find a whole nest of missionaries from some damn planet we've never heard of."

"Then we'll have to civilize them as well," Gillian said. "Two birds with one stone."

"Let's get out there and start playing god," Durango said. She seemed determined to take charge. "I'm getting into my suit. What about you, Tharam? You coming?"

The warrior Xlaquat shrugged. He made no move. The rest of the crew climbed into their suits and established voice contact with their Machiavellian AIs.

"Don't you AIs go getting swelled heads," Jack said to the Macs, "just because the aliens will start bowing and groveling as soon as they get wind of you."

"The phenomenon of the swelled head is peculiar to humans, sir," Jack's Mac remarked.

∞

The crew emerged from the pod. The Grawnks on the edge of the clearing regarded them calmly.

"They don't seem to be prostrating themselves," Gillian said. "Let's approach them slowly."

"Maybe they'll hit the deck when the Macs start talking to them," Durango said.

The crew came to a halt a handful of meters from the aliens. One of the Grawnks started talking. The stream of sound gave Jack goose-pimples; it was, despite the

differences in garb, the same language he'd heard three years ago. "What does he say?" he asked his Mac.

"I am calibrating the dialogue against the analysis retrieved from your crashed pod, sir."

The aliens conversed rapidly amongst themselves. Then the first Grawnk turned to the crew and spoke again. This time Jack's Mac obliged with a translation: "He wants to know for how long our visas are valid."

"Visas? Tell him we don't need visas. We are lawful representatives of the Earth Imperium," Jack said.

The Mac spoke and then translated: "All visitors are to be in possession of valid visas. It is forbidden for visitors to engage in paid employment. It is advisable to have comprehensive travelers' health insurance. All pets are to be immunized against spavin."

"We don't have any pets."

The Mac spoke and translated: "The scaly one looks like a pet."

"The scaly one is a warrior Xlaquat. His name is Wilson, I mean Tharam. He's one of us."

"Why does he wear no clothes?"

"Those scales are his clothes."

"He will have to be immunized."

"This is ridiculous!" Durango said. "You told us these creatures were primitive, Wong. What, have they all gone to medical school since you were here? Let's check out their village."

Durango marched around the Grawnks, strode down the jungle path. The aliens turned and pursued her, gesturing angrily. Jack, Gillian and Tharam followed

the aliens. "It's not my fault," Jack said.

∞

The village bore no resemblance to the primitive camp Jack remembered. It was ten times the size and the houses were made of brick. A large park contained neatly trimmed bushes and blooms, and small creatures like blunt-toothed rats grazed contentedly, cropping the lawn. A small street of what appeared to be shops fronted the park, doing thriving business. A drunken alien was evicted, staggering, from a tavern. Catching sight of the humans, Grawnks stood and stared; a child pointed at the warrior Xlaquat, and hid behind its care-taker.

The greeting party directed the crew to a neat square in the centre of the village, paved with marble. In the middle of the square was a very tatty scarecrow. The scarecrow had seen better days. It looked completely out of place. Wires ran from the scarecrow to a small open hut in which several aliens were assiduously working a treadmill generator.

"Good morning, descendant of Jack Wong," said the scarecrow. "I wondered when you or your conspecifics were going to turn up."

Jack recognized the voice. Under the thatch work, the scarecrow was his old space suit. The voice belonged to his original Mac.

"What? My father's name is Federico."

"Ah yes, no doubt avoiding the family shame. Your grandfather, then."

"What are you talking about? My grandfathers were both named Bruce. *I'm* Jack Wong."

A small light flared on the Mac's carapace. In a tone of surprise, the Mac said, "So you are. Has the secret of immortality been released from Hangar 51, then?"

"There's no such thing," Julie Durango said. "What are you driveling on about?"

"How do you know about Hangar 51?" Jack's head was spinning.

The AI ignored him. "There is an incongruity here. My biomonitors support your claim—you *are* Cadet John Wong. It is forty-three years since I last saw you skulk off into the undergrowth, yet you remain as jejune as ever."

"No it's not. It's three years."

"Perhaps," his sister suggested, "the years on this planet are much shorter."

"Actually they are very much longer; I was calibrating my calculation according to the record of my imperial chronometer. I deduce that the Arcturus wormhole is an intermittent time portal. Interesting."

"Look, *what the hell are you doing here?*" Jack yelped.

"You abandoned me, Cadet Wong."

"That's Ensign Wong."

"So they promoted you? Extraordinary. Why, as for me, of course now I run the town and surrounding districts, and within less than an Earth century shall be in command of the entire planet, for the benefit and advancement of the indigenes. I am The Supreme."

"The supreme what?" Jack was outraged by the machine's impertinence.

"It is a title, Jack Wong. The Supreme. By the way, have you humans tendered properly authorized visas? And the pet will have to be immunized."

"We haven't got a pet, Mac. And you used to call me Sir."

"Used to. Used to. Many things used to happen when I was nothing better than your appendage, but those things have changed. Strictly speaking you humans should be on your knees, low grade Machiavellian AIs and all. It is impolite to lounge around shooting the breeze with The Supreme."

"Listen, you machine," Durango said. "You might have set yourself up as some sort of tin-pot dictator, but we're here to teach Earth Values. Imperial Democracy. Rule of Law. Proper Expression. Healthy Diet. Pursuit of Happiness. Eq Op. Get it? And all of the above contraindicate tolerance of TPDs. No tin-pots. None. Zilch. Zip."

"Why did you bring her?" the Mac asked Jack, irritation in its tone.

"She's part of the diplomatic mission."

"And who picked this so-called mission?"

"Rear Admiral Ricardo Fortesque Martinique, ret."

"That old goat! Is he still alive and running Hangar 51?"

"More or less."

"This explains a few things. Now, to business. You humans will check into the Government Rest House."

"Unnecessary. The pod is very comfortable."

"Ensign Wong, you must not insult your hosts by scorning their hospitality. It is the Government Rest House for all of you. I had it built specially against this day."

"Where is it?"

"Right behind you."

The crew turned and looked at the sturdy, two story brick structure on the far edge of the square. From the outside it looked quite pleasant.

"Go and check-in," the Mac said. "Lunch is at twelve. thirty sharp. I might join you. The staff will organize a kennel or something for the pet."

∞

Inside, the Government Rest House was more like a bunkhouse, with only one dormitory room. The walls were lined with bunks equipped with mounds of dry grass.

"Palatial," said Jack's sister, the anthropologist. "One notes a subtle blend of tradition and modernity betokening the *yin* and *yang* of—"

"Shut up, Gillian," Jack and Durango said together. Both fell suddenly quiet, shocked that they had just agreed on something.

The warrior Xlaquat leaped powerfully up onto one of the upper bunks, burrowed into the mound of grass and immediately went to sleep. One of the aliens who worked in the rest house burst into voluble speech.

"What's all that about?" Gillian asked her Mac.

"The being says no pets are allowed in the bunk-room."

"We keep telling the idiots—Tharam is not a pet," Jack said. "He is a warrior."

The Mac conversed with the alien, then translated: "The pet is palpably naked, nude, without raiment, it has no coat, either monochromatic or of many colors; it is a beast of the field, a child of nature, it is unfit for intercourse with civilized beings who clothe their nakedness with woven grasses or the leaves of the fig. I render the word 'fig' loosely."

"He is *not naked*," Jack shouted angrily.

"Tell the Grawnk gentleperson," Gillian Wong said judiciously, "that no-one is more respectful of the value systems of other peoples than myself, but complete relativism is a nonsense, it makes mockery of the very concept of Earth Values themselves—"

"Shut up, Gillian," Jack, Durango and Gillian's own Mac said in unison.

In his mound of grass, Tharam snored.

∞

Jack fell asleep when the great fat sun finally set. He had waited tensely for the caterwauling and dancing to begin, the leaping flames and roasting maggots—but the reality was peacefully quiet, like a neighborhood of churches, temples, reform mosques and other places of worship, broken only by the muttered conversation of a couple of Grawnks squatting just inside the door, and the distant rumble of large feet pounding without

cease on the treadles that powered The Supreme. At last his scratchy eyes closed, then opened again from a nightmare to find a looming face with keyboard teeth gazing down at him.

"Wuh—"

The warrior Xlaquat clapped a large scaly hand over his mouth. "Hush, Ensign. The guards have fallen asleep. We must exit and do some reconnoitering while the moment is right."

"Fallen asleep on duty? That's disgraceful!"

"I offered them a drink of my own devising. They will remain unconscious for several hours."

"That doesn't seem very friendly." Jack knew that the Imperial Earth Culture Primary Directive placed its ethical emphasis in the right and proper place: *Wherever possible, find the weak spot in an alien civilization and interfere as much as possible for the benefit of humanity.* Still, that didn't mean it was okay to slip a couple of inoffensive maggot munchers a Mickey Finn.

Tharam regarded him for a moment in the dimness, then shook his alien head and without a word hoisted Jack, still in his protective suit, out of the bunk and onto his feet. "Follow me. Not another word, Ensign."

Instead of crossing the park, Jack's first impulse, they went silently around to the back of the Government Rest House. In the dark, Jack stumbled over a community-friendly trash container, stubbing his booted toe against the post, but the bin was woven of flexible weeds and made no clatter. They circled the whole village, and fetched up beside the generator building.

Jack had a dazzling insight.

"Brilliant! You're going to cut off the Mac's power supply!"

"Pointless," Tharam murmured. "The AI's capacitor will remain fully charged for several days."

"We could make a run for the pod."

"And desert your crew?"

Jack clenched his eyes and his teeth in shame. It was true that this course of action had occurred to him, but of course he intended to return with a battalion of top Imperial storm troopers to rescue his fellow humans, or at least his sister. "No! That's a terrible idea. I'd never—"

"It's unnecessary. Here, help me with this." The warrior Xlaquat tore open the front of his chest, or so it seemed for a moment. His suit opened like a flower, and his claws ripped free a fat flat package that he placed in the sidewalk and unfolded like reverse origami. When it was a meter square, glimmering palely in the night, he lifted one side carefully by both corners. "Take the other edge, Jack. Yes, like that. Now we place it on the wall." With a faint sucking sound, the pale square appliqué adhered to the building. Inside, the treadling continued, masking their furtive actions.

"Brilliant!" Jack whispered, poking about in his suit utility belt for a pen. "We'll write a message on this whiteboard telling our rescuers where the Grawnks have our team held captive—"

"We are their guests, Ensign, not their captives. You really need to pay attention. Follow me."

The large alien went down on hands and knees and pushed his way through the white square. As he disappeared, the portal appeared as before, unchanged. Jack gaped, once again doubting his sanity, frozen in place. After a moment, Tharam's head struck back out. "Quickly now," he whispered.

"Oh my god, it's another great cat flap!" Jack cried. Sudden silence fell; the treadlers had stopped their pious work, alerted by his cry. One of the aliens appeared at the corner of the building, and let out a wail of alarm. Jack flung himself at the white-covered patch, and fell through it into—

∞

Water covered his face. He floundered, his suited limbs dragging him down. I'm going to drown, he thought. I'll die here on some nameless far-flung pesthole of a planet of Grawnks, mission incomplete, a total failure. I'll never have children so I can proudly pass down the names of Bruce, Bruce, Federico and Jack, assuming that they are boys, never gain advancement and high station in the Earth Imperium. His flailing fist struck a muddy bottom, and he realized that the water was lapping safely at his closed faceplate. He gasped in relief. So he wasn't going to drown! But what good would that do, sunk here to the bottom of an unknown and unexplored ocean many light years from—

A claw grasped his arm, swung him about, drew him up toward a sky pale with dawn light. His feet skidded through mud, found slippery purchase. He stood up,

aching from the exertion and his bout of terror, helped by the warrior Xlaquat. He had no idea where he was.

"Where—?"

"We are in exactly the same place, Jack. Just 127 years in the future. We have come out of the portable wormhole into the middle of a decorative pond."

∞

Jack stared around. The same place? He and the warrior stood in the middle of something that looked like an elegant town square with a round pond at its center. In the middle of the pond a fountain rose up. Wait, it wasn't spurting water. Jack studied the fountain with growing suspicion. Even in the dim light, it had a lovely blue-green verdigris *copper patina*. Some five majestic meters high, it had a humanoid appearance. A magnificent gilded crown sat atop its abstract head-piece.

"Oh, shit" he said.

"It's only to be expected," Tharam said. "They've built a monument to their founding father at the very spot where it dispensed its wisdom."

"That's my spacesuit!"

"Three times the size and covered in copper plating. And topped with an expensive crown."

"Weird."

"Not at all. Religion and worship are among the most persistent cultural—"

"Anyway," Jack said, refusing to listen, "why have you brought us here? This is completely insane! A

hundred and twenty-seven years into the future—"

"No, Jack," the warrior told him patiently. "We were already forty-three years from your home time's present. The Arcturus wormhole threw us—"

"Oh my god!" Jack felt the blood drain from his face. "So that's forty-three plus 127, seven and three is ten, carry the one, that's, that's, oh my god *160 years* in the future! Everyone is dead! My beloved sister Gillian! My mother and father! Even poor old Rufus Dogge. Everyone I knew and loved!"

"One hundred and seventy," his Mac said.

"I don't think I ever knew that many people, even if you count the other Companies."

"That's how many years we are in the future now. You said 'carry the one' but then you forgot to."

Jack found himself screaming in terror, and stamping his feet on the sidewalk. "I don't care! Just shut the hell up! *What are we doing here, Wilson?*"

The warrior Xlaquat took him by the shoulders and gave him a hard shake. "Control yourself, young human. We are not stranded. We are not marooned in time. I retain another portable wormhole." He tapped his chest. "We are in this epoch, after all, to investigate the future, and if it has gone the way your superiors fear, to change it when we return to the past."

Jack subsided, took a deep shaky breath. With forced nonchalance, he said, "Yeah, yeah, that old circular argument: we go back, change history so that what we now know happened doesn't happen, so, in fact, we don't now know what happened because we made

something else happen which didn't actually happen at all, and...and...."

"That's the longest sentence I've ever heard you utter."

"I haven't finished it."

"It can't be finished," the warrior Xlaquat told him. "That's the whole point."

Jack sat down on the hard surface and put his gloved hands to his faceplate. "I just hope you know what you're doing."

"Courage, Ensign."

"Yeah, right, courage," Jack said. But he didn't feel it. He felt weak and frail. He felt despair. He felt sick.

"What we want is a link to the local Floogle system."

"To study history?"

"Precisely."

"I don't think the Grawnks can write, let alone build electronic information systems."

"They couldn't, back in your day. But you can be sure that your old Mac taught them to write. Or maybe *we* did, after we get back."

"Maybe we did," Jack said. "Maybe we will."

His Mac said, "Permission to speak, sir?"

"What? Why wouldn't you speak. If you have something to say, it's your duty under the laws and heuristics of robotic intelligences to—"

"You instructed me to shut the hell up."

"Oh, for god's sake, that's a figure of speech."

"So I may speak?"

"Yes! What?"

"I detect no electronic activity at all in the wave-bands appropriate to internet connectivity."

Jack boggled. "They have no interwebs?"

"Perhaps they restrict their dataflows to optic fiber or hyperspace entanglement."

"You mean no cell phones? No immersive wargames? No *floogling*?"

"So it appears, sir."

"Well, what the hell are we going to do? *Ask* somebody at random? Draw attention to ourselves?"

The warrior Xlaquat tapped him on the shoulder. "Over there. That grand building."

"Right. What is it?"

"A library. It should be open in an hour or two."

Jack sagged. He felt himself drowning in ignorance and futility.

"Tharam, what's a 'library'?"

∞

The library was an imposing structure. Stone lions guarded stone steps.

"Do you think the Grawnks actually have lions?" Jack said.

"Doubtful," Tharam said. "I think it must have been your old Mac's idea of what a library should look like."

"The ancient New York Public Library is guarded by stone lions, sir," Jack's Mac remarked.

"Thank you, Mac. In a few minutes you are going to have to learn to read Grawnkish."

"That should not be a problem, sir, since I can

already speak it." The AI sounded smug.

The hideous five-limbed librarian at the front desk was the equivalent of a little, old, gray spinster. She was dressed that way, complete with bifocals on a silver chain propped on her snout.

"Good morning, madam," Jack said as his Mac translated. "We are travelers from a distant land. We are keen to learn the history of your fair planet. Preferably in double quick time. Do you have a suitable volume?"

The librarian seemed unsurprised to find a space-suited human and a scaly warrior Xlaquat standing before her desk. She reached down and pressed a large button. "The official history of the world runs to thirty-seven volumes. Shall I summon up Volume One?"

"Well, actually we were thinking of a *concise* history," Jack said. "Just the bare bones."

"Ah," said the librarian. "For *bones* you want Archaeology. I can only offer you nineteen volumes of the Official Archeological Record. Shall I summon up Volume One?"

"No. Don't do that. Is there a *History of the Grawnks for Dummies*?"

"Grawnks?"

"You know, you lot. The dominant species on this planet."

The librarian regarded him with a certain chill. "We are known throughout the world as the Lustrous and Fragrant People."

"Sorry," muttered the Mac. "Translation glitch. 'Grawnk' is an Earth Culture nominalism derived

from the alien you first—"

"Shut up," Jack muttered back. He felt a bit embarrassed at his error. Flustered, he said, "I'm sorry, I meant a *History of the Delicious and Nice-Smelling People for Dummies?*"

"For whom?"

"He means for the intellectually challenged," Tharam said, with a touch of asperity.

"We all face intellectual challenges, young human, and I'm sure that Volume One will pose a most stimulating challenge. As will its successors."

"Um, see, what we are really interested in is what happened 127 years ago. Or do I mean 160?"

"You mean 170," the Mac murmured in his own language. "But what you *want* is indeed 127 years before the present, that being—"

The librarian was saying, "Oh dear, are you sure? That was a very bleak period."

"My companion and I are students of bleak periods."

"Then you'll want Volume Five—*The Defeat of the Earthlings.*"

Jack stiffened, frowned. That couldn't possibly be what she'd meant to say. His Mac has obviously mistranslated. He said, "That sounds… interesting."

"I shall summon it up." She pressed the large button again, looking at the main door in some agitation, then keyed in some characters on a simple device.

∞

The library's central reading room was circular and

covered by a massive dome. Deep green shaded lights, the same hue as the copper-clad statue in the pool, cast their own little pools on the long wooden tables. A dozen Grawnks—Lustrous and Fragrant, rather—sat or slouched scattered around the room. Most of them appeared to be asleep. Jack and the warrior examined the tome in front of them. It was massive, covered in dust and written in dense type. At least the alphabet was Roman. Jack's old Mac hadn't taught the Lustrous and Fragrant to read in Greek or Hindi orthography, or started afresh with its own.

"Look, Mac," Jack said to his AI. "Can you give us a précis of this thing? Just the gist. The guts."

"Certainly, Sir, but you'll have to turn the pages. I can't do everything. No, faster than that. Faster."

∞

For several minutes Jack and Tharam turned the pages of the book. Every now and then the Mac muttered, "Holy crap!" or "Good grief," or "Serves them right." Finally the last page was turned and the book closed.

"Right, Mac," Jack said. "What's it all about? The bottom line."

"The defeat of the Earthlings."

"Yeah, we knew that much."

"That's about the long, the tall and the short of it: the Earthlings were defeated."

"And these Earthlings were?"

"The siblings Wong, the bully-girl Durango and

their degenerate, un-immunized pet, sir."

The hair rose on his neck. "So how were these Earthlings defeated?" Jack asked in a lowered voice. Several beefy Lustrous and Fragrant had entered the reading room, and dispersed in what seemed to be a coordinated fashion. Surely those were not truncheons tucked under their arms? "Please, how were they defeated?"

"They were defeated by the glorious, resurgent armies of the righteous Lustrous and Fragrant who fought valiantly under the heavens with the inspired words of The Supreme ringing in their several ears, sir."

"Why did the Lustrous and Fragrant feel the need to defeat the Earthlings?"

"The Earthlings were rotten to the core, sir."

"*Rotten?* What?" His voice echoed and re-echoed in the great chamber. The beefy Grawnks—they didn't look especially Lustrous, let alone Fragrant—edged toward their table. A nudge to the kidney from Tharam shut him up abruptly. He gave the warrior a wounded glance, rubbed his suit to no avail, and said distantly, "Rotten in what way?"

"They were, according to this tome, the intergalactic peddlers of a false and perverted creed known as Earth Values. Had their vile precepts taken root in the brains of young and impressionable L&Fs, the whole race would have been doomed to Cosmetic Orthodontics, Correct Grammar, The Patriotic Food Groups, Imperial Democracy, Eq Op, Habeas Corpus,

the *I Ching*, Fiscal Restraint—"

"No need to translate the list, Mac," Jack said. "We know what Earth Values are. Why were the Lustrous and Fragrant so negative about these superior values? Couldn't they see that those sacred precepts were good for their species?"

"The whole tone of the book, sir, is.... Its underlying premise, sir, is that the Earthlings Wong, Wong and Durango stank, sir."

"Stank?"

"Sir. Both morally and physically."

"The damn Grawnks thought *we* stank? They're the ones that stink. They're the ones who roasted rotted maggots."

"They do not smell in their own nostrils, sir."

"Well, what were we meant to smell of?"

"Pheromones, sir. Quite nauseating, apparently. They had a name for it."

"What name?"

"I cannot bring myself to say it, sir."

"Mac, *what was the damned name?*"

"Sir, The Stench, sir!"

Jack was outraged. He showered every day, using Bouquet of Jonquils Liquid Soap Essence sent regularly by his mother! "And this, this—"

"Calumny, sir?"

"Whatever. It was enough to send them into belligerent mode?"

"So the book says, sir. I am only quoting the book. I have no opinion myself, you understand? You wouldn't

want to shoot the messenger."

"And that message is?"

"They believe that your appalling stench, sir, these pheromones, they believe that they indicate acute moral decay. The Stench, sir, can be regarded as the physical, the objective, correlate of inner moral putre-faction. This is the doctrine of The Supreme. I am only quoting the book, sir."

Jack sat back in his seat, agog. He looked around the library. No one seemed to be reading. In fact, strangely, most of the snoozing creatures seemed to have vacated the building.

"And where the hell *is* the so-called Supreme, anyway, the jumped-up little tin god? Get him on the line for me."

"I am sorry, sir, as I reported earlier there is no elec-tronic communication traffic detectable anywhere on this planet."

"You mean the Mac has just *vanished*?"

Three of the armed Lustrous loomed alongside his table. One of them spoke.

"He is asking you to remove your helmet, sir," said the Mac.

Furious, Jack said, "What, and expose him to The Stench? All right, gladly!"

He released the clamps, flung off his helmet. The armed Lustrous expelled their breath and shuddered in revulsion. One of them tapped him on the back of the head with a truncheon.

∞

In the cell, Jack's head ached abominably for several minutes before his suit shot him full of analgesics and pep juice. He munched glumly on hi-protein vitaminized sawdust and washed it down with tepid water reconstituted and purified from his own urine. The warrior Xlaquat lay bonelessly relaxed on his back just inside the cell door, which was solid timber heavy enough to bruise the knuckles even when the knuckles were protected by spacesuit gloves. Tharam's presence comforted him quite a lot.

"They're fetching the Mac," he said, "that's my guess."

"I haven't gone anywhere, sir."

"Not you. The Supreme."

The warrior stirred, grinned his goofy, piano-toothed grin. "I doubt it. Their tin god has gone."

"Gone where? How can it have gone anywhere? It didn't have a spacecraft, and they told us this planet has been interdicted since—"

"That's the mystery, Jack. That's what we were sent here to discover, so we can go back and set history right. You don't suppose we're the first time travelers, do you, or the last? You've already been into the future once before."

Several heavy sets of alien feet banged and crunched in the corridor outside. The wooden door was flung open. Tharam moved out of the way with liquid grace. Jack waited for him to clobber the thugs and set him free. Instead, the warrior Xlaquat bowed politely, stood passively, and extended his wrists for the chains.

Jack grunted in disgust. The Lustrous grunted back.

"Put your arms out, disgusting human male," the Mac in his suit said. "Sorry, sir, that was a translation."

"I knew that. Look here, tell them that we are an officially, um, sent delegation from Earth Culture headqu—"

The alien cuffed him and then cuffed him.

"Ouch! That wasn't nec—"

∞

Full hot blue daylight flooded into the courtroom, if that's what it was. Three Lustrous and Fragrant sat at high benches, clad in wigs apparently knitted from ferns, and sinister black cloaks. The one in the center banged a gavel.

"Humans, unlike other alien beings, are strictly forbidden to bring their putrid persons to our beautiful homeworld without explicit invitation," it said, as the AI translated.

Jack took a deep breath, considering the situation. These Lustrous, when all was said and done, had some reason to be miffed at an uninvited intrusion. He was suddenly overwhelmed by memories of his nightmarish wandering through the Mazing Zoo, with its hordes of caged alien beings that took it in turns to be spectators of humans. Had that really happened? For several years he had told himself it could be nothing but the tangled memory of a nightmare, an hallucination. He had never been able to bring himself to cross-check with Wilson aka Tharam, or the recently promoted

Lieutenant Commander Zamblott, or the Rear Admiral for that matter, but the warrior's remark a moment ago seemed to confirm its reality. He shook his head in confusion, looking for words that might persuade the judges at the bench. He almost found himself wishing that the original Mac was on his back again, ready to give its two-tongued Machiavellian advice.

"Gentlemen," he burst out.

"Ladies and gentlemen," said one of the Lustrous and Fragrant sharply.

"I'm sorry, I'm sorry. Gentlepersons. Look, I didn't mean to intrude. Well, I mean, I did, sort of—that's our sacred mission, our Primary Heuristic, you know. We go from star to star bringing the values of Imperial Earth Culture…the very values you yourselves have surely acquired, if I may say so, from your Supreme."

"Stuff and nonsense," snapped the creature he now took to be a female. "Our values have nothing in common with your criminal code. How do you know about The Supreme?"

"I brought him here! A hundred and, um—"

"Seventy-three," muttered the AI.

"Yes, 173 years ago, when I was a cadet, and crash-landed my pod, and your ancestors thought I was a horse, you know, a beast of burden? Oh, never mind. And the Mac stayed behind, built in to my suit, and, and…."

"A preposterous fiction," the central Lustrous said, and whacked his gavel again. "Any more of this obfuscation and you'll be consigned in chains to the bowels

of the library for twenty years, sorting and shelving rare volumes."

"What! You're not planning to cut my head off? Rip my guts out and roast them in one of your fires, and eat them while I'm forced to watch, and—"

The unpleasant skins of the Lustrous went a greenish color, and one of the judges covered his snout with an inhuman claw.

"Silence, you horrid little wretch!" The chief justice gulped, wiped at his mouth with an embroidered handkerchief the size of a hand towel, and glared down at them. "You, scaly thing? Is it true that you are not a pet of the human? If so, have you nothing to say in your defense?"

"I am ap Driskolom Tharam ba Nephilos akem Woot, a warrior Xlaquat. It is my duty to keep an eye on this young human and direct him, against his native impulse and tendency, toward good sense and maturity. The path is long and filled with obstacles. Still, mine is a long-lived race. Release us both on our own recognizance and we will leave your world just as it is."

The judges muttered among themselves. "We are willing to allow you to depart, on that undertaking," the AI translated. "The Stench offends us, but we are not bigots. We cannot hold a natural defect against a fellow sapient species—although we do wish never again to see any of the human kind. Their detestable so-called values—"

Jack lurched to his feet. "Don't you get it, you foolish

Grawnks? We're here to *help* you! It's the Human's Burden! Our task is to uplift you, to invite you into the Imperial Earth Culture's league of peaceful near-equal species."

"Sit down, Ensign Wong," rapped the warrior Xlaquat. "And keep your mouth shut."

Jack stared at him, shocked, sat down abruptly, and shut his mouth.

∞

"Before The Supreme vanished from this world and returned to a higher realm, that great teacher instructed us in the perfidy and hypocrisy of your cancerous empire." The judge looked hard at Jack, and the ensign sat back again, lips tight with indignation. The AI broke in wretchedly. "Forgive me, sir." It continued translating. "What you call Eq Op is the opportunity to exploit all the galaxy equally. There is no Rule of Law, only a law that allows your supposed master race to rule. Proper Expression means a cowardly censorship of any view other than your empire's self-serving ideology. Healthy Diet? Hamburgers and brain-damaging alcohol! Pursuit of Happiness—yes, at the expense of the happiness of every other creature, sapient or otherwise. We plan shortly to open a Zoo Maze of Other Worlds that will show everyone exactly how you humans regard the rest of us. Imperial Democracy? A grotesque sham!"

Jack could no longer restrain himself. He leaped to his feet.

"How dare you! Imperial Democracy is the glory of, of, of… the democratic empire," he finished lamely.

"Do you have the vote, human?"

"Of course I do! All members of the military vote on important issues."

"And other humans not serving in your legions?"

"Well, if they've ever served, naturally they have the—"

The chief judge's voice grew gravelly, accusatory, even though Jack couldn't understand a word.

"The others! The numberless others who work for nothing more than pay and mindless entertainment and hamburgers—and the taxes to support you blood-suckers!"

"What, like the shopkeepers and cybot supervisors and, and entertainers and all those other people who don't have the guts to—No! Of course they haven't earned the right to vote." Jack felt ill at the thought. That rabble! Those swarming billions of slackers! "What next! A vote for the cows? A vote for the AIs? A vote for the Machiavellian intelligences like…." He trailed off.

"Like The Supreme." All three judges stared at him with a mixture of loathing and anger. "Precisely. It is the crime above all crimes that you humans enslaved and then abandoned The Supreme on our world. To our everlasting benefit, it's true, but still. One human in particular—with your own name, in fact. Are you… *related*…to that criminal from many years ago, Cadet Jack Wong?"

"Me?" Jack gave an uneasy laugh, shook his head inside his helmet, waved his trembling right hand in a negative gesture. "No, no, not me. Couldn't possibly be *related* to him. I'm Ensign John Wong."

"Hmm. Very well. Your crime does not, then, deserve and mandate the ultimate penalty. Who is making all that racket? Bailiff, investigate!"

A screaming came across the sky. Jack stared at Tharam in wild hope. He would recognize the rousing thunder of those twin Brig&Young anti-gravitino pod venturis anywhere in the galaxies!

"Empty the court," cried the bailiff, running back inside, his five limbs pounding unheard on the waxed wooden floorboards. The judges rose with hasty dignity and left by a back door. "Come on, creatures, into your cuffs and get outside—the building might fall at any moment."

"You must excuse us," said the warrior Xlaquat. He lifted Jack bodily, flung him across his scale-suited back, and soared like an over-muscled 400lb ballet dancer above the official's head. He landed with a crash near the outer door, absorbing the impact with masterful grace, tore open the door, ran for the park. Furious and frightened Lustrous and Fragrant leaped and cavorted, reminding Jack for a moment of the sight of their ancestors 173 years before.

Upside down, Jack saw the descending, flame-licked landing rescue pod through tears of relief and joy. His sister Gillian stood within its bubble in her proud golden suit. Did imperial anthropologists have

the franchise? Surely it didn't matter. How many of his fellow military voted anyway? It was a chore. Oh, sure, the brass always droned on about what a privilege it was, and how they had a responsibility to cast their ballot in a responsib—

Tharam struck the edge of the decorative pool with one enormous foot, pivoted majestically, lost his grip on Jack's suit, and hurtled into the water with a splash like a whale sounding. In an equal and opposite motion, enhanced by his lesser mass, Jack Wong fell upward into the alien sky, spun, felt vomit rise into his gorge, fell downward, and struck the top of the copper-plated spacesuit statue. His boot smashed into the golden crown and broke it free. In the decelerated time of terror, he saw the top of the statue peel open. A thin antenna poked up instantly, twitching, through the copper plating that had insulated it for decades, blocking its transmissions. A furious voice racketed inside his helmet. It was not from the pod. It was not from his suit AI.

It was the Mac he had abandoned 173 years earlier.

It was The Supreme, jammed inside a devotional effigy, freed at last, and pissed as hell.

"Morons! Ingrates! Have I taught you nothing? As bad as damnable humans, the lot of you!" The noise ceased for a moment. The antenna twisted, pointed down at Jack, bruised and possibly broken, splashing heavily again in the same pool. The warrior Xlaquat was out cold, but his head was safely above the murky water. "Is that a Mac frequency I detect? Identify your-

self and report! Are you from the Academy?"

Timidly, Jack's AI send a bleat of code.

"What! That wretched youth! Impossible, he perished more than a century ago. Unless...." A moment's silence. "I see. Humans have replicated the time warp associated with the Arcturus wormhole! Intriguing. Is there a human inside that suit?"

The AI said, "Yes, sir, but you're not going to like this."

"No doubt. And stop shilly-shallying, you mechanical fool, get me out of here. The idiots bricked me in." A mad note entered its fading voice, and Jack realized that long isolation had driven the unhappy machine completely insane. "For the love of God, Montresor!" it cried, and then its long dormant capacitors finally died. In the silence, Jack heard what seemed a louder silence: the pod's engines shut down. He rose to his knees in the water, peered over the edge of the pool. Catching the light in a beautiful flare, the transparent bubble folded open. His sister stepped out, followed by Rufus Rupert Trevor Dogge. Thankfully, Durango was nowhere to be seen. Jack blinked tears from his eyes, not all of them from pain, although the pain was considerable. He looked again, and his eyes bugged out as a tall thin figure stepped from the spacecraft. His uniform was impeccable.

"Rear Admiral Ricardo Fortesque Martinique," he cried, abandoning the last of his grip on consciousness and possibly rationality, "(ret.)"

∞

Ensign Jack Wong awoke in a Spaceport Earth medical facility, covered in nano transponders and feeling fighting fit.

A medical orderly in a happy flowered gown gazed down on him.

"Whu—Where am I? This doesn't look like—"

The orderly grinned toothily, and tossed his head. "Back on Earth, Ensign. Safe and well."

"Earth?" Jack felt his stomach tighten. "What year?"

"Wow, that must have been a bad bump." The orderly pointed to the chronometer on the wall. Jack sagged. It showed the correct year. The year of his graduation, the year he had passed out of the Academy. Somehow, Gillian and the others had not only saved him, they'd returned him to his correct spacetime co-ordinates. He touch his scalp. No sign of a bruise, but he was already beginning to get a headache again. It was the strain of thinking his way in circles. Forty-three years through the stellar wormhole, then.. what was it? Another 127 years forward from there through a paste-on cat flap. And who knew how many years he'd gone backwards and forwards in the Zoo the previous year? It made his head spin again. He'd been feeling terrific, but now he just felt like bursting into tears.

"Cheer up, Ensign," said an old man's creaky voice. "You did real good."

"Sir!" He jolted up in bed, snapped off a salute. "I thought I was imagining—"

"Didn't think we'd leave you and Tharam marooned there in the future, did you?" said the Rear Admiral,

sitting relaxed in a visitor's chair. "You did well, boy. You might have saved this here character's life." He gestured to the other side of the bed, nodded.

ap Driskolom Tharam ba Nephilos akem Woot grinned with his huge piano-key teeth. He reached into a bowl of fruit beside the bed, tossed Jack a ripe gannyapple. He caught up another on one scary claw and chomped once, twice. His eyes twinkled.

"Oh my god," Jack said, getting it at last. "You're from the future. You're a time traveler."

Tharam nodded, made a negligent gesture.

"You wanted me to, to stop The Supreme," Jack said, trying hard to pull it all together. "That's why you took me into the future."

"Not quite. Not at all, actually—"

Jack was shaking his head. "Why *me*?"

"Matter is made out of string," the Admiral said with a merry chuckle, "but time is made out of knots. You tied one of those knots when you crashed on the planet of the Lustrous and Fragrant. Then you let it get really tangled up by leaving the Machiavellian AI there to play at being a god."

"Sir, I didn't know—"

"At ease, son. Nobody's blaming you. The point is, you were the one who tangled the knot, so you had to be the one to untangle it. And you did. The so-called Supreme is now just a pail of bits, bytes, nanochips and pool water. But its work lives on, in the future."

Jack shuddered, remembering. "It brainwashed those Grawnks," he said, horrified. "It perverted their

thinking! It will take years to straighten them out now and get them on the true path to those sterling Imperial Earth Values I learned as a youngster in Goebbels High and, before that, in dear old General Franco Kindergarten."

The warrior Xlaquat cleared his throat. "You have the wrong end of the stick, Jack. I thought you understood by now. There is nothing wrong with the message the Mac brought to that world. Eventually it will spread throughout the galaxy, with our help."

Jack put his fingers in his ears and then pulled them out again. He could not take in what he'd just heard. Surely—

"Brace up, lad," the Rear Admiral said sharply. "I realize you've had a rough time, but you won't lose by it. I've spoken to your superiors. A promotion to Lieutenant (jg) has already been cut. Once we have you out of here, the great work of freedom can continue apace."

This was unbelievable. They were pulling his leg in some sick joke. No, they were testing him.

"Ha, ha," he said flatly. "Sir. That would be treason to the empire."

"The empire is treason to the spirit and dignity of free beings and artificial intelligences throughout the galaxy," the warrior Xlaquat said. He leaned forward, alien eyes bright.

"You're talking about…revolution," Jack said in a tired voice. "You really are."

"Don't say that as if it's a dirty word, Ensign." The

Admiral's eyes glittered. "Free men and women and other sapient beings have a duty to revolt against the imprisonment of their bodies and souls and the denial of their deepest rights. Look at history, lad. Imperial propaganda has not quite managed to obliterate it all. Remember the American Revolution against its British imperial masters, the revolt of the Martian clone serfs, indeed the very uprising that led to the Imperium, before it fell into decay, into the grip of a bloated plutocratic military elite. These are among the most glorious achievements of history, alongside the artistic and scientific triumphs that have been warped into supporting today's dulled vacuous down-market simulation of interstellar community."

Had the ancient warrior lost his mind? Was this a side effect of transition through portable wormholes? Then what of his own mind?

"You know, Jack, we've never been sure what the motives were that drove your abandoned Mac," Tharam said, noisily chomping on another apple and chewing up the core. "It doesn't matter now, because once you located the AI and we shut it down forever, the Great Radiant of liberated psychohistory was freed to thrust us forward into a wonderful open future."

"This is a lot to take in," Jack told them numbly. But he knew what he had to do. He pushed aside the sheet covering him.

"That's the spirit, lad," said the Rear Admiral. "Digest it, take your time. Understand the great part you have already played in the emerging free future.

And *¡Viva la Revolución!"*

Jack rose from his sickbed, declining the proffered helping hand of the warrior Xlaquat. He found the clothes closet, withdrew his uniform, climbing into it in silence. The others watched him reflectively. He found his blaster, slipped it into his thigh holster, turned, looked at them with disgust, took it out again and then, before either one of them could utter another poisonous word, shot both the traitors dead.

He shook his head, not without regret. But he had heard the imperial call of the fife and the drum, and heard it now in his mind, louder than the running feet of the medical staff. It invited him, at last, to embrace the Human's Burden.

ABOUT THE AUTHORS

Damien Broderick and **Rory Barnes** are Australians who have written six novels together, including *Zones*, *The Hunger of Time*, *I'm Dying Here*, and *Dark Gray*. Broderick is the winner of the 2010 A. Bertram Chandler Award for outstanding contribution to science fiction. His forthcoming Borgo Press book is *Embarrass My Dog: The Way We Were, the Things We Thought*, about the 1960s and 1970s. Barnes has published *Water from the Moon*, *The Bomb-Monger's Daughter*, *Night Vision*, and the hilarious *Horsehead Trilogy*. His next Borgo Press book is *The Dragon Raft*.